"Do you like my mountains?" Zack asked from behind her.

Kira whirled to face him. He leaned against the sliding glass doors, watching her. He was dressed simply in jeans and a sweater, but the casual clothing did nothing to diminish his aura of controlled power.

"I didn't mean to startle you. I wanted to see you, Kira," he said softly. "I couldn't sleep for thinking about you last night."

Her eyes widened. "Why?"

"You persist in questioning the obvious." He smiled, his eyes bright with amusement. "If I tell you, do you promise to blush again?"

"How unkind of you to notice. I can't help blushing, but I'm working to overcome it."

"Don't! I like your blushes. Every time I see the heat beneath your skin I want to reach out and touch you, feel the heat, the softness, the silk."

She tried to but couldn't look away from him. That maddening color rose to her cheeks. Her lips trembled as she smiled. "I'm not usually like this. You make me a bit nervous. I don't know if I'm equipped to handle a man like you, Zack."

There was a sudden glint of mischief in his eyes. "It's a skill I expect to enjoy teaching you. It will be an exquisite pleasure being handled by you." He held out his hand. "Starting now, Kira. Please, love, come to me. . . ."

WHAT ARE *LOVESWEPT* ROMANCES?

They are stories of true romance and touching emotion. We believe those two very important ingredients are constants in our highly sensual and very believable stories in the *LOVESWEPT* line. Our goal is to give you, the reader, stories of consistently high quality that may sometimes make you laugh, sometimes make you cry, but are always fresh and creative and contain many delightful surprises within their pages.

Most romance fans read an enormous number of books. Those they truly love, they keep. Others may be traded with friends and soon forgotten. We hope that each *LOVESWEPT* romance will be a treasure—a "keeper." We will always try to publish

LOVE STORIES YOU'LL NEVER FORGET
BY AUTHORS YOU'LL ALWAYS REMEMBER

The Editors

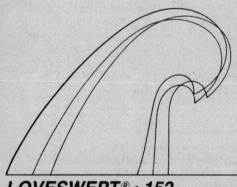

LOVESWEPT® • 152

Iris Johansen
Everlasting

BANTAM BOOKS
TORONTO • NEW YORK • LONDON • SYDNEY • AUCKLAND

EVERLASTING

A Bantam Book / August 1986

ISBN 0-553-21766-6

Published simultaneously in the United States and Canada

PRINTED IN THE UNITED STATES OF AMERICA

O   0 9 8 7 6 5 4 3 2 1

One

"There he is! That's Zack Damon's car!"

With a nearly inaudible swoosh the Silver Shadow Rolls Royce drew to a halt before the auditorium. Photographers and reporters converged on the car with an eagerness they hadn't displayed for either the rock star who had just gone into the lobby or for the governor, who was still lingering outside to shake hands with his constituents.

The reaction of the press was perfectly understandable, Kira Rubinoff thought as she carefully drew the hood of her black velvet cloak forward to shadow her face. Both the star and the politician constantly made themselves available to the media, while Zack Damon was almost as publicity shy as Howard Hughes had been. Perhaps wariness of the media was a trait shared by billionaires in America, where as much attention was paid to self-made tycoons as it was to royalty in Europe. Yet Damon was known to be exceptionally reclusive in that elite set of the reclusive. The only public functions he had attended this year were selected benefits and special fund-raisers for various American Indian welfare groups. By poring over newspaper and magazine articles in The New York Public Library reference room, Kira had learned a great deal about him, including the fact that he'd be attending this benefit. The Damon Foundation was a sponsor of the Indian Heritage Center; the Center had used Zack Damon's name and clout to pull in the galaxy of stars who were to perform tonight.

As the door of the Rolls was being opened by a uniformed chauffeur, Kira quickly stepped back into the shadowy mouth of the alley leading to the stage door. It was highly unlikely that Damon could spot her even if he were looking for her . . . which, most definitely, he was not. After all, he didn't even know her. Still, it didn't hurt to be cautious. In this, her first glimpse of the flesh-and-blood man, she definitely wanted to see, yet remain unseen.

Power. The word struck her like a blow as she watched him get out of the car. Quiet, effortless power. She knew from the articles she'd read that he was in his thirties, but he could well have been any age. He was tall and broad shouldered. Long, sleek muscles lent grace to the movements of his big body. By contrast, his face seemed brutal: black brows slashed across his forehead to frame eyes as night-black as his hair, and broad Slavic cheekbones ran parallel to a jawline that was firm and determined. That face, that composed, strong face revealed a man who had endured and waited, gathering about him forces only he could control.

He wore a black tuxedo with the casualness of one accustomed to evening wear, but who was still impatient with its necessity. And, she thought, he was handling questions from the reporters with much the same attitude he displayed toward the wearing of the tuxedo: accustomed, but impatient. Kira listened closely, not really interested in Damon's answers so much as the manner in which he gave them.

"You're not with Mallory Thane this evening. Does that mean your liaison is over?"

"I have no liaisons."

"It was reported that she stayed the weekend with you in Acapulco."

"I have no liaisons."

Blunt, impassive, soft-spoken.

"Is it true that the AirFlow merger is being fought by the unions?"

"You'll have to ask them."

"Are you half or quarter Apache, Mr. Damon?"

"Half. My grandfather was shaman of his tribe."

"You're also illegitimate. Right?"

That question obviously struck a nerve. Damon's gaze fastened on the reporter who'd asked the question. The man took a hasty step backward. "Yes, I'm both a bastard and a half-breed," he said softly. "Considering what I've made of myself, I'd say that speaks well for being both. And just what have you made of your life to date, Mr. . . ." He looked at the man's press badge. "Carter?"

The reporter didn't answer. He bent his head

hastily over his notebook. Kira didn't blame him for avoiding Damon's challenging stare. She wasn't sure she would have had the courage to look Damon in the eye at that moment. How unnerving to experience the lethal swiftness with which he could change from neutrality to attack.

Another reporter spoke up. "You've been fighting for better education and employment opportunities for Indians for the last twelve years. Though I'm sure it's very laudable, don't you believe that a lot of what the American Indian experiences today is due to resentment of his savagery in the past?"

"No," Damon responded quietly. "I think his present situation is due to the fact that he wasn't savage enough."

But *he* would have been savage enough to hold what was his, Kira thought. She shivered. Oh lord, what had Marna gotten her into?

A small, graying man with a wide smile on his plump face had gotten out of the front seat of the Rolls. He was also dressed in a tuxedo, and he spoke as he stepped between Damon and the reporters. "Mr. Damon will give you a statement about his involvement with the Indian Heritage Center during the intermission. I'm afraid you'll have to excuse him now. It's time for him to go to his box."

He plowed ahead, running interference for Damon with the media, fending questions as fast as they were fired. As they entered the lobby the crowd closed around them, hiding Damon from Kira's view.

She drew a deep breath and tried to relax the muscles of her shoulders. Until Damon had vanished from sight, she hadn't realized how tense she'd become while observing him. Maybe it would have been better "to beard the lion in his den" without any prior knowledge of him. At least she wouldn't have been nervous. Heavens, how silly she was being. She'd been dealing with powerful people since she was a child, and shouldn't be intimidated at all by Zack Damon. But then, she had never been a supplicant before. Begging for help for the first time was bound to put butterflies in anyone's stomach, she reassured herself.

In a swift gesture of bravado, she tossed the hood of her cloak back. A mass of riotous auburn curls tumbled over her shoulders. She stepped quickly out of the alley and walked briskly down the street to where her taxi was waiting. The time for hiding in the shadows was over. It was time for her to act with her usual forthrightness and to accomplish her task.

Perry Bentley firmly closed the door of the box, shutting the reporters out. His genial smile vanishing, he turned to his employer and spoke rapidly. "Jansen called on the car phone just after you got out. Princess Rubinoff was in the crowd in front of this auditorium."

Damon's gaze flew to Bentley's face. "Here?"

"At the mouth of the alley. She was wearing a black velvet cloak, obviously trying to go unrecognized."

"You're sure?"

"Jansen followed her from her hotel. He couldn't be more sure."

Zack turned away to hide his expression from

Perry, whose eyes revealed unabashed curiosity about this situation. It would take little encouragement, Zack knew, to cause Perry to unleash that curiosity in a barrage of questions. Perry wasn't at all intimidated by him, as most other people seemed to be, and most of the time Zack appreciated that quality in his assistant as much as his loyalty. But not in this particular matter. "How did she get here?"

"A taxi. She had it waiting for her around the corner from the theater."

"A taxi!" Zack muttered a brief, explicit curse that caused Perry to lift his brows in surprise. "What the hell is her brother thinking of to let her go running around the world without security?"

"Princess Rubinoff has the best security that money can buy," Perry reminded him mildly.

"But good King Stefan doesn't know that."

The savage tone of voice Zack used caused Perry's eyes to widen. He hadn't heard Zack speak so harshly in the seven years he had been working for him. Zack was usually quite soft-spoken. There was no need for a man to raise his voice when everyone was more than eager to listen.

"How stupid can the man be?" Zack snarled.

Perry shrugged. "I've heard he's not the most enlightened of monarchs, but then Tamrovia is so small, maybe he doesn't have to be."

"Get on the phone and call Jansen back. I want to know where she goes in that taxi."

Perry nodded and slipped out the door of the box.

The houselights went down; a spotlight was thrown on the velvet curtain at center stage. Zack sat down in a plushly padded chair in the rear of the box, his eyes fixed unseeingly on the master of ceremonies, who walked into the spot.

Why was Kira here? Zack wondered. She had been only a few yards from him and he hadn't even known it. After all these years she had finally been almost close enough to touch. He could have crossed the space between them in seconds. No, the space between them couldn't be measured by distances. Even if he had crossed those few physical yards, they would still have had a very long way to travel to meet one another. He mustn't get overeager just when it was most important to keep control. He knew about patience and control. Events could be shaped and worlds conquered by a man who possessed those two qualities. He drew a deep breath and concentrated hard to regain a sense of peace and tranquility. It took longer than usual to accomplish, but he had succeeded by the time Perry came back to the box.

"Well?" he asked his assistant.

"The taxi is heading north on the Santa Catalina Highway toward the Santa Catalina Mountains. If her destination is the one I think it is, she's going to have one hell of a taxi fare."

"My lodge." It was a statement, not a question.

Perry nodded. "It makes sense. According to the report, she flew into New York City from Tamrovia yesterday afternoon. She made one long stop at The New York Public Library and then hopped on another plane. She arrived in Tucson today, the day you just happened to be here, showing up outside this theater. Now she's making a beeline in the direction of your lodge on Mount Lemmon." He cast Zack an inquiring glance. "Do the security guards at the gatehouse have her on their list for automatic clearance?"

"No." It had never occurred to Zack that she might ever come to him. "You'll have to call security and set up clearance for her. Have Juana make her comfortable until I can get there. Tell one of our people to check her out of her hotel and bring her luggage to the lodge. She'll be spending the night."

He was tempted to leave now and to hell with the gala, but he had promised his full support of the event to the people at the Heritage Center. He would stay until the intermission was over and then have Perry help him slip out through the stage entrance. It wouldn't hurt to let Kira wait. With her volatile temperament she probably couldn't bear to wait for anything or anyone, he guessed. Her nerves would be tuned to a fine pitch and that would be to his advantage. Unlike her, he had had to wait for everything he'd ever wanted.

Perry was once again opening the door of the box. "I'm surprised her name's not on your clearance list," he said, clearly puzzled. "She's been protected by your security system all the time I've been working for you."

It's been far longer than that, Zack thought, his expression passive as his gaze flicked idly to the musical extravaganza now taking place on the stage. "There's no reason why she should be on the list. We've never met." The corners of his mouth turned up slightly. "Yet."

Getting into this house had been too easy, Kira realized as the door of the library closed behind the

Indian housekeeper. Billionaires had tight security and strangers, even titled strangers, simply didn't walk right into their homes. But she had. Why, she hadn't even been asked for identification! Both the guards at the gatehouse and the Indian servant who had opened the door had acted as if they expected her. Well, maybe they did, Kira thought. Perhaps Marna had managed to invoke one of her spells to make all doors open for Kira. That wasn't likely, however, since Marna had problems with even short distances and it was a very long way from Tamrovia to Arizona. No, Kira's visit wasn't a surprise.

Or rather, a visit by a *lady* wasn't a surprise. Kira had learned from those frustratingly scanty articles she'd read in the library that a lady's presence in Damon's house and bed were not unusual. A number of beautiful and well-known women were rumored to have been his mistress at various times over the years. She didn't doubt even one of those rumors now that she had seen him. A raw sexuality radiated from him along with his aura of power, and both of those fierce, elemental qualities in him had disturbed her. Oh, dear, it would be just her luck to interrupt a lovers' rendezvous and have Damon toss her out before she even had a chance to talk to him. Well, he'd just have to wait to take Mallory what's-her-name to bed. Kira's problem was a good deal more important than Damon's immediate sexual gratification.

She might as well make herself comfortable, she decided. There was no telling how long it might be before Damon showed up. She shrugged out of the black velvet cloak and tossed it on the long couch before an open fieldstone fireplace. She smoothed the amber chiffon of her gown with quick, trembling fingers, then realized how the gesture betrayed her nervousness, and deliberately stilled her hands.

Good heavens, she was acting as if *she* were Damon's date for the night instead of that gorgeous actress. Why had she worn this gown anyway? Maybe it would have been better to be cool and businesslike. She had instinctively armored herself for the coming interview in the only way she knew: by making herself look as alluring as possible. Enough men had told her she was attractive for her to believe that it was at least partially true. Some of them hadn't even had anything to gain by telling her, so maybe . . . Oh, what difference did it make? She wasn't in some kind of competition. Damon either would or would not do what she wanted.

She settled herself comfortably on the couch and gazed around the room, searching for a clue to the personality and character of the man who used it. The contemporary furniture was all in earth colors—browns, beiges, and rusts. The lines were clean and comfortable yet austere. No clues there. The paintings on the walls also told her little. The works of El Greco, Delacroix, Titian, Russell, and Remington hung side by side. Damon evidently had varied and definite tastes. The painting over the fireplace, hung in a position of prominence, could be presumed to be a favorite of Damon's. Perhaps it revealed something of the man.

She got up to read the title on the frame. *Song of the Talking Wire* by Henry Farny. It was a strong, lonely picture depicting an Indian who was no longer young, standing by a telephone pole in a desolate western landscape. He had been hunting and his kill was draped over a horse standing with as much dignity as the Indian man. There was a weariness as well as a strength about the old Indian. The weariness could have been the result of the hunt or the bewildering encroachment of white man's civilization, represented by the telephone pole against which he was leaning.

Had Damon, living in a world of two cultures, felt that same conflict? If he had, he obviously had resolved the conflict. There had been nothing discouraged or bewildered about the man who had stepped out of that Rolls tonight. He was the most confident and aware man she had ever seen. She sighed. The mystery of Zack Damon couldn't be solved by studying this painting. She felt a twinge of disappointment as she sat back down on the couch and curled up in the corner. She had always found that understanding made even the most intimidating people more approachable, but there was no reflection of any human foibles in Damon's surroundings. The room was as much of an enigma as the man himself. She would just have to wait until Damon himself appeared on the scene and then play it by instinct alone.

She wearily rubbed the tense muscles in the back of her neck. She had been traveling constantly and sleeping very little during the last few days. Her vitality was usually so great that flying didn't faze her. It was only because her nerves had been stretched to the breaking point that she had been unable to overcome jet lag. Her nerves were still taut and she was growing more hyper with every passing moment. She had to try to relax or she would be in no condition to face Damon when he finally arrived. She closed her eyes and forced herself to take deep, steady breaths. There, that was better. She could feel the slightest ebbing of tension. If she could keep it up, perhaps she would be relaxed and refreshed when the time came to face Zack Damon.

Kira was asleep. Of all the states in which he had imagined he might encounter her, sleeping wasn't one. She was curled up, her head pillowed on the arm of the couch, her hair splayed in a fiery mass against the beige velvet of the cushions.

He stood looking down at her and felt an odd tightness in his throat. She seemed infinitely small and vulnerable at this moment. When she was awake she exuded a vitality and vivaciousness that was incandescent, making her appear larger, stronger. But now her lips were pink and crumpled looking, their look of sensitivity enhanced by being slightly parted. Her nose was small, her cheekbones high; her triangular face was more fascinating than pretty. When she was awake her features were mobile and constantly alight with laughter and *joie de vivre*, but now sleep revealed a curious helplessness about her. He'd better enjoy that helplessness while he could, he thought, amused. When she lifted those long lashes, her sapphire eyes would hold challenge, not vulnerability, and her boneless grace would be transformed into a soft curvaceousness that could raise a response in a man to rival the heat of an Arizona summer.

He would not wake her. There was no hurry. He felt a deep contentment at the sight of her, relaxed and abandoned in this room, in his home. He moved swiftly to the easy chair across from the couch and sat down. He had no need to draw control and patience to him now. She was here. He would sit and watch her while she slept. His waiting game was almost at an end.

Two

How could she have believed that his dark eyes were enigmatic, Kira wondered. They were gentle and wise and so deep that she felt lost in them. No, not lost. He would never let her be lost. He knew exactly where he was and his place in the scheme of things. If she clung to him tightly, she could never be lost again. He had a beautiful mouth too. She hadn't noticed how well shaped it was when she had first seen him.

The faintest smile curved those lips. "Good evening, or perhaps I should say good morning? It's almost three o'clock, you know."

She looked around for a clock and was immediately struck by the strangeness of her surroundings. Oh, Lord! She bolted upright, swinging her legs to the floor. "I'm sorry. I didn't mean to go to sleep." She brushed unruly curls away from her cheeks, saying impulsively, "I haven't had much rest in the last few days and . . ." She drew a deep breath. This was ridiculous. She was acting like a frightened child. She straightened with royal dignity and lifted her chin. "How do you do, Mr. Damon. I'm Princess Kira Rubinoff."

"You'll forgive me if I don't stand and bow, Princess Rubinoff," Zack Damon said in a lightly teasing tone, "but I've had a rather tiring day myself." He stretched his long legs out before him. He had taken off his black tie and unbuttoned the collar of his shirt but was still dressed in the tuxedo he had worn at the gala. "I assure you I had no intention of committing lese majesty."

She made a face. She'd probably sounded as stiff-necked as Stefan, she thought ruefully. "Insult this royal person in that way all you please. I'm afraid that whenever I get flustered, I fall back on those pompous manners drilled into me from birth. Please call me Kira. Everyone does." She smiled. "Besides, economically speaking, you're far more royal than I'll ever be. I have a wardrobe allowance, but little else. Stefan keeps me a virtual pauper."

He lifted a brow. "Really? I had no idea Tamrovia was so poverty-stricken. Is the purpose of your visit to enlist foreign aid?"

"Foreign aid . . . well, yes. In a funny way, I guess that is why I'm here." Her smile faded and her gaze narrowed thoughtfully. "You know who I am. I wouldn't have thought you would. There are so many princesses running around Europe these days."

"But you're an exceptionally newsworthy princess. It isn't every princess who dances in Rome's Trevi Fountain at midnight."

"I wasn't dancing in it," she said indignantly. "The *paparazzi* misrepresented the episode. Actually, when I tossed my coin in the fountain I was so furious that I made a horribly bloodthirsty wish against someone who was annoying me at the time. Then I had second thoughts and decided he didn't really deserve such punishment."

"So you tried to get your coin back and undo the curse?"

"Well, I didn't want to take chances. You never can tell what works and what doesn't."

"No?" There was a glint of amusement in his eyes. "Were you also trying to undo a curse when you pushed the Spanish pretender to the throne off the dock at Corfu?"

"Hm-m. It seemed an effective way to get his pudgy hands off my body and keep them off. He appeared to be intent on adding this princess's scalp to his belt." She closed her eyes. "Oh, dear, I shouldn't have said that, should I? I didn't mean to cast aspersions on your Indian heritage. So much for the foreign aid." She heard a deep chuckle and her eyes flicked open. "Thank heaven you have a sense of humor."

"I'm serious about my heritage, not fanatic." He smiled faintly. "You'd be a most desirable prize whether you were a princess or not. I can't say I like the literal image of your scalp dangling from a warrior's belt, though."

Kira felt oddly breathless. There was something . . . She breathed deeply. "I assure you that José wouldn't have wanted the scalp—or anything else—if I didn't have the title. I didn't realize that my escapades had been so well publicized in the States." She shrugged. "Maybe it's because I went to college here. Well, all of that business with fountains and docks took place when I was much younger. I'm not so impulsive anymore."

"I'm glad old age has tempered you," he said solemnly. "You're how old now? Twenty-two or twenty-three?"

"Twenty-three," she said, frowning. "Your newspapers seem to be very informative."

"Not really. There was actually very little regarding your background. You're Princess Kira Rubinoff, your parents are dead, and you're under the guardianship of your brother, King Stefan of Tamrovia. You have another brother, Lance, who lives in Sedikhan and is an extremely gifted artist. I have a few of his paintings, by the way."

"Isn't he wonderful? He painted a few portraits of me when I was a child, but hasn't used me as a subject since then. He says he's waiting until I've 'set.' " She wrinkled her nose. "Makes me sound about as appealing as watery Jell-O."

"You seem to be quite fond of him." His eyes narrowed. "Why didn't you ask him for help? I understand he's very well off."

"He's closely linked to Alex Ben Raschid, the ruler of Sedikhan. I can't involve Sedikhan in my problems again. The last time I nearly caused a diplomatic incident. I'm trying to keep the knowledge of this mess from everyone in Sedikhan." She nibbled at her lower lip. "It's not entirely a financial problem. That wasn't what I meant."

"This sounds intriguing," he said slowly. "Or it

would if I had any idea what you were talking about. Suppose you clarify matters by telling me just why you've decided to pay me a visit at this unusual hour."

"Well, I couldn't be sure of being able to contact you at any other time or place. I figured since you were in Tucson, you'd stay a day or two to conduct business." She gestured vaguely. "You have gold mining interests or something here, don't you?"

He wondered what the board members of the gigantic Shaman Copper Company would say to such an offhand reference. "Or something. It seems you've done a little research on my humble enterprises."

She gave a distinctly unladylike snort at that blatant understatement. "I looked you up in the library. I had to find some way of tracking you down. You're an elusive man, Mr. Damon. And Marna was no help at all."

He went still. "Marna?"

She gave a sigh of relief. "You remember Marna? I was afraid you'd forgotten her, and that would have blown everything. It's been so many years."

"No. I remember Marna Debuk very well."

"She said you would, but then she clammed up on me." She ran her fingers distractedly through her curls. "I've seen her be maddeningly inscrutable with other people, but never with me."

There was hurt as well as bewilderment in her expression and Zack had a sudden impulse to cross the space between them and take her in his arms to comfort her. His hands on the arms of the chair tightened until his knuckles showed white.

Not yet. "She loves you very much. I'm sure if she thought it best to—"

She impatiently held up her hand. "I know. I know. It's just that I'm so worried about her. I need all the help I can get, and she picks a time like this to become mysterious."

"I think you'd better start at the beginning."

"Am I being incoherent?" She grimaced. "It's one of my worst faults. Verbal chaos." She bit her lower lip. "The beginning. I don't have any idea how much you already know. Blast Marna, anyway."

"The beginning," he repeated softly.

"Well, you do know Marna is a Gypsy and a member of one of the largest tribes in Tamrovia. It's a long-established custom for a member of her tribe to serve in the royal household in each generation. Marna became my nursemaid when I was born and has been with me ever since." Her expression softened. "My parents and Stefan never had much time for me and Lance was in Sedikhan, so there was really only Marna. She was everything I needed or wanted."

"That's quite an accolade."

"She's quite a woman." Uneasy, Kira hesitated. "Quite an unusual woman. She has certain . . ."

"Powers," he suggested softly.

Her breath came out in a little rush. "You know about that?"

"I know that she told me she could work spells and sometimes see what others could not."

"And you believed her?"

"My grandfather was a shaman and I spent a good deal of my childhood alone with him in the hills. I know that power exists."

"That simplifies things a bit. I could see myself quite futilely trying to explain about Marna's powers. Well, anyway, my brother Stefan is a bit of a *chitka*."

"*Chitka?*"

"Sorry. It's a Tamrovian word. It means fool or idiot. Stefan decided when I was sixteen that I should make a marriage of state, and he tossed me to the lions, or rather to the title hunters. He forced me into contact with every head of state and powerful tycoon in the world."

"Not every tycoon," Zack corrected quietly.

"If you hadn't been hiding in the mountains playing Howard Hughes, I can assure you that you would have topped Stefan's list. Stefan was very determined." Her lips tightened. "But so was I."

"Hence, the Corfu dock incident?"

She nodded. "Marna and I managed very well at first. Sometimes it was almost amusing. Then, last year, Stefan got impatient with the game and decided to end it. He imprisoned Marna to pressure me to give in."

"Rather a drastic solution. Don't you have a habeas corpus law in Tamrovia?"

She shook her head. "It's an absolute monarchy. Stefan claimed she was aiding me by casting harmful spells on prospective suitors."

He lifted a brow. "And was she?"

She shrugged. "Nothing very important. Maybe a minor rash now and then." She bristled. "And they deserved it."

"I'm sure they did."

"Well, naturally I couldn't just leave her in prison. Clancy Donahue, Chief of Security of

Sedikhan, and I broke her out and smuggled her across the border to Sedikhan."

"I've heard of Donahue. I once tried to hire him as head of my security force."

She shook her head. "Clancy would never leave Alex Ben Raschid or Sedikhan."

"I found that out. Pity. He's a remarkable man. Go on. I gather your troubles weren't over when you reached Sedikhan."

"They should have been, but Marna was miserably unhappy in Sedikhan. She has very close ties to her tribe and she missed her people. So I went back and tried to pacify Stefan."

"Pacify?" All humor vanished from his face. "How?"

"I thought if I was pleasant to some of the men Stefan wanted me—"

"Pleasant." The word was razor sharp. "Is that a euphemism for sleeping with them?"

Her eyes widened with surprise. "Of course not. I told you, those kinds of men really were interested only in my title. I'm not exactly a sex symbol, you know."

She honestly believed what she said, Zack realized. She didn't know that her extraordinary vitality alone was a sexual draw. "I'm afraid I forgot," he drawled while wondering how a woman in her position could have remained so damned naive.

"Well, it isn't important. It didn't work out anyway. I'm not very docile and things happened . . ."

He was sure he would be fascinated to know about those "things," but at the moment he needed to get her to the crux of the story. "And?"

"I returned to Sedikhan to wait for Stefan's temper to cool. I was going to try again, but Marna was impatient. She wanted to see her people, if only for a visit. So I smuggled her back across the border into Tamrovia."

"Quite a busy border."

"It's not amusing. Stefan had men waiting at the Gypsy camp when we got there." She frowned. "I don't know how he knew that we'd be there. No one in Sedikhan would have betrayed us."

"So Marna is in prison again?"

"She's under guard in an apartment close to mine at the palace. Stefan thought it would be more difficult for me to bribe the palace guards." She added dryly, "Not that I would have had the money to do it."

"So that's the present situation?"

She hesitated. "That's not quite all of it. About six months ago Stefan appointed a new adviser, Sandor Karpathan. I think he might be manipulating Stefan by pitting us all against each other to further his own ends."

"Why do you think that?"

"I don't know. He's always very polite and charming. It's just that there's something—"

"Woman's intuition?"

"Woman's *judgment*," she corrected. "Besides, Marna doesn't trust him."

"Ah, the final condemnation." He held up his hand as she opened her lips to protest. "I'm not mocking you or Marna, Kira. I believe in instincts. I've relied on my instincts all of my life. Is Karpathan the principal reason for this sudden urgency?"

She nodded. "I was nearly frantic. He frightens

me. I didn't know what to do. Then Marna sent for me and told me about you."

His stillness took on charged tension. "Really? What did she tell you?"

"Not nearly enough," she said crossly. "Only that when you were a boy in your teens you traveled with her tribe one summer. She said she'd met you when she'd left the palace and gone back to the caravan to nurse her mother for a few months. I understand she's kept track of you through the years, she feels strongly that if anyone can get her out of Tamrovia, it will be you. She said you and a man named Nick O'Brien went into Said Ababa right after the revolution and freed some of your employees who were being held hostage. Is that right?"

He nodded. "But a war torn country is a good deal easier to manipulate than a stable government like Tamrovia."

Her eyes were suddenly wide with fear. "Does that mean you won't—" She stopped. "She sent you a message. I have no idea what it means, but she said you would. She said to tell you it was the time of the *mondava*."

His heart skipped a beat and then started to pound so hard he felt a little dizzy. He had to struggle to keep his face expressionless. "*Mondava* is a Tamrovian word. I learned only a little Tamrovian that summer. You should know better than I what it means."

"It means 'the bonding.' "

He shook his head. "Not quite. In Marna's dialect it means the 'forever bonding' or the 'everlasting bonding.' "

Her eyes lit with sudden interest. "You *do* know what she was trying to tell you."

"Yes, I know."

She waited eagerly. Then, when he failed to elaborate, she grimaced. "But you're not going to tell me either, are you?"

"Perhaps if you wait a little longer, I won't have to tell you."

"Damn, now you're being as cryptic as Marna. I *hate* to wait." She jumped to her feet, walked across the room, and stood restlessly beside the fireplace. "I can't bear double-talk. It drives me out of my mind. Are you going to help Marna or not?"

"Just what are you asking of me? Do you want money?"

"I don't know. I suppose it will take money. You should know better than I, considering your experience in Said Ababa." Her hand closed tightly on the oak edge of the mantel. "I want her out of Tamrovia and safe, and I don't want this to happen ever again."

"How much do you really care?"

Her voice dropped to a whisper. "I care more about her than about anything in the world. I love her so very much."

He was silent a moment, his gaze fixed on her face. "What did Marna say to you when she sent you to me?"

"She said you were a *disek,* one of the exceptional ones." She hesitated and then added slowly, "She said I should put myself in your hands, do whatever was necessary to bring you to Tamrovia."

"And just what do you intend to do?"

"Exactly what she told me to do," she said simply.

His lips twisted. "You're very meek and obedient all of a sudden. And you're making a total commitment."

"Don't you think I know that? I'm scared to death you're going to ask me to hijack a plane or something. You're a complete stranger to me."

"Yet you're willing to obey blindly a woman who hasn't set eyes on me for over fifteen years."

"I've trusted Marna all my life. She wouldn't do anything to hurt me. I've got to hang on to that certainty."

His gaze forthrightly met hers. "What you're asking will be very difficult. It will take money and time. I have quantities of the former and absolutely none of the latter. I'm in the middle of a merger. It just may go down the drain if I neglect it during this crucial period."

Her lips drooped with disappointment. "You're not going to help me."

"A faulty conclusion, Kira. I'm merely stressing the point that if I make certain sacrifices, I'll expect compensation."

She shook her head. "I told you I don't have any money."

"But you do have something else I want."

"The title? You want to marry me and have a princess to add to your status?" She felt a sudden jolt of disappointment. Somehow she hadn't expected such a superficial response from Damon. "All right, but I—"

"Not the damn title," he said harshly. "Why the hell do you think that's all there is to you? I don't need to marry a princess to show the world I've made it. *I* know I've made it, and that's all that counts."

She should have realized. She would have realized it if she'd thought for a moment instead of reacting immediately. "I'm sorry." She smiled shakily. "I seem to be apologizing a good deal tonight. I didn't mean to make you angry."

"You didn't make me angry. I guess it was natural for you to think that of me." His eyes narrowed on her face. "I suppose your brother Stefan would consider me beyond the pale as far as bloodlines go. I know nothing about my father, except that he was a white man. It was the only thing my mother would tell my grandfather about him."

"You're probably right about Stefan," she said frankly. "I told you he was a *chitka.* But your money would endow you with a very tolerable patina in his eyes. What difference does it make? You said you didn't want to marry a princess anyway."

"Yes, I did, didn't I?" He rose to his feet. "But I said nothing about not wanting to take Kira Rubinoff to bed. Do you think Stefan would object if you took me as a lover?"

She gazed at him blankly. "Sex?" She didn't know how she got the word out. Her throat had closed and she couldn't seem to catch her breath. "You want to have sex with me?"

He slowly shook his head. "I want to be your lover. I want to sleep in the same bed you do; I want you to let me make love to you whenever and however I wish, for as long as it pleases me." His voice lowered to a velvet softness. "I believe I can guarantee it will please you as much as it will please me."

She didn't doubt it for a minute. Sexual magnetism radiated from Zack Damon in an almost visible aura. She felt a languid heat begin to flow through her at just the thought of his intimate touch. "Why?"

He smiled. "I don't believe a woman has ever asked me that question when I asked her to go to bed with me. The answer seems self-evident. However, I can make it much clearer, if you like."

She moistened her lower lip with her tongue. "We've just met. I'm not unattractive, but I don't exactly exude feminine allure, either. You're willing to jeopardize a merger to go to bed with me?" She shook her head in bewilderment. "I don't understand this."

His rare smile widened to warm his dark face. "Perhaps I have peculiar tastes. You happen to appeal to me very much, and I can afford to let the merger slide. You had no problem at all believing I would want to marry you for status, and you agreed to that without a second thought. Why are you having a problem with the idea of being my mistress? The position would be much more advantageous for you. You'd have your freedom and still get what you want from me."

"I don't know." She gazed at him, frowning. "I think it's because I thought I had something to offer you in the title. This is entirely different." Her hand left the mantel and her fingers raked distractedly through her hair. "Look, I don't know anything about being a mistress. It isn't very sophisticated of me to admit it, but I'm a virgin. I don't know how to please you, dammit. One time and you'd probably drop me like a hot potato."

"I doubt that." He suddenly chuckled, his dark eyes dancing. "Undoubtedly I'd be magnanimous and give you a second chance. Practice makes perfect."

"You don't mind—"

"I don't mind anything but this inferiority complex you appear to have acquired." He rose lazily to his feet. "You agree to my terms. I agree to yours. Deal?"

She nodded. "I guess so, but—"

"Hush. Never quibble after a deal is made. It's very unprofessional." He was walking toward her.

"I don't know much about deals and—"

"I do." He was standing beside her and she felt suddenly smaller and more womanly than she ever had in her life. His warmth was surrounding her and she could catch the scent of soap and musk and something vaguely woodsy. "I'm an expert on making deals. I'll teach you. The first thing you should know is the difference between a takeover and a merger by mutual consent." His index finger touched the pulse point on her neck. It rested lightly, as if testing the pounding of her heart. She felt the throbbing go wild beneath his touch. She could tell by the sudden flickering in his dark eyes that he felt it too. "I've always preferred mergers by mutual consent. It makes for a much better assimilation of assets."

His finger was slightly unsteady on her flesh. Was she having such an effect on him? It seemed incredible, but they were so close she could see the erratic throbbing in his temple. "Now?" she whispered.

"What would you say if I said yes?"

Her gaze met his steadily. "I don't know very much about deals, but I know about meeting obligations to the people I love. You'll be giving me far more than I will be giving you. Why should I object if you want to collect in advance?"

"I can see we're going to have to do something about your sense of self-worth." His finger moved from her throat to her lips and she experienced a burning sensitivity that startled her. The tip of his finger gently smoothed the fullness of her lower lip and the same tingling followed in its wake. Her lips felt soft and swollen. "You're ripe for a takeover, Kira. If you don't start negotiating, we may both be lost."

"But you said—"

"A preliminary foray to seek out weakness."

Her gaze was clinging helplessly to his. Lost. She had a fleeting memory of the complete trust she had felt in him at her first moment of awakening. If he were lost with her, she wouldn't be afraid. "Zack . . ."

He closed his eyes. How many times had he imagined her saying his name in just that way? The scent of a light floral fragrance wafted to him from those tousled auburn curls. He knew Marna blended a perfume for Kira from gardenias and the very lightest touch of cinnamon. But how could he have guessed the effect it would have on his senses? He'd be drunk and dizzy with the scent of the perfume and of her when he buried his face in her hair and moved over her to . . . He blocked the thought, but it was too late. His groin was a solid ache of throbbing need and his stomach was knotted with tension. She was here and willing. Why not?

"Zack?" It was a puzzled thread of sound.

The *mondava*, dammit. Marna had sent Kira to him. She had expected him to take her. He knew that, yet there was something wrong about rushing her to bed as his body dictated. No, not wrong, but not right, either. And it must be very, very right.

He opened his eyes and then wanted to close them again. Her blue eyes were mist-soft and questioning and her lips were slightly parted. He had never tasted her, never really touched her, never threaded his fingers through her hair and pulled her head back so her throat arched and her breasts pressed against his chest. His gaze dropped to the full swell of her breasts encased in the amber chiffon. It would take so little to brush that veil of amber aside. She drew a deep, quivering breath and her breasts lifted and then fell. He knew she was aware of what he was thinking. She wouldn't stop him. He would take his time and pleasure her. He would roll her nipples between his thumb and forefinger. His lips would pull gently and his tongue would— Hell!

His finger dropped from her lips and he took a step backward. "Anticipation," he said thickly. "It makes the pleasure infinitely sharper. I think we'll indulge in a few more preliminary forays before we conclude the merger."

She should have been relieved. He was a stranger. She didn't really want— Yet, if she didn't really want him, why was she experiencing such a sinking feeling of disappointment . . . as if some long-awaited present had been moved suddenly out of her reach?

Her lips still throbbed where he had touched them and her breasts felt as sensitive and swollen as if he had touched them as well. It was crazy. She had met attractive men before, yet never felt this volcanic sensual upheaval. She tried to smile. "Whatever you say. It's your deal."

"Yes." He turned away abruptly and crossed to the desk. "I'll ring for Juana to show you to a guest room for the night."

"I'm checked in at the Hilton in Tucson."

He smiled. "No problem. I'll have someone check you out and pick up your bags. By the time you've showered and had a hot drink, they'll have delivered them to your room. I want you here tonight. We'll be leaving for Tamrovia in the morning."

Her head lifted swiftly. "We will? You can manage to get away that soon?"

"You said you wanted Marna out immediately." He pressed a button on the console on the desk. "I'll get her out. I'll work on the details and discuss them with you tomorrow on the plane. It shouldn't be too difficult to establish ourselves at the palace, if Stefan has no objection to me as your lover."

"Won't he suspect something? One day I'm threatening to clobber him with his stupid royal scepter, and the next I show up with a lover no one knew about."

"With his own scepter?" he asked, amused. "Now that is lese majesty. Don't worry. We'll concoct a plausible story of a previous meeting. To prepare the way, I'll contact my public relations man tonight and have him leak the story of our flaming love affair to a few well-known gossip columnists in Europe, along with the fact that you spent the night here. You needn't trouble yourself about any-one questioning the validity of our affair once we reach the palace." He paused. "It will be clear even to the most casual observer that we're sharing a bed."

Color flooded her cheeks. Damn, not only a virgin, but a blushing virgin. How unsophisticated could one get? She turned with relief as Juana appeared at the door. "Oh, well, I didn't think we should signal our purpose too obviously. Good night, Mr. Dam—Zack." Lord, five minutes ago she had been on the verge of tumbling into bed with him and she wasn't even comfortable calling him by his first name.

He had caught the slip and there was suddenly a twinkle in his eyes. He bowed with mocking panache. "Good night, Princess Rubinoff. Juana will serve you breakfast in bed at nine. I'd like to be at the airport by eleven-thirty. I hope that will suit your highness's convenience?"

As if he cared. If it had happened to suit *his* con-venience, he would have been in bed with her. "Fine," she said softly. "I'll see you in the morning then."

The amusement on his face faded as he watched the door close behind her. It had been touch and go toward the end whether he'd let her leave, and he wasn't at all sure he hadn't been a damn fool to do it. He was so aroused that he was sure he wouldn't sleep at all, and it was definitely questionable whether or not he'd be able to play the game he'd set for himself. Anticipation of having Kira had gone on too long for him. He would try to go very slowly and get her accustomed to him, one intimacy at a time, but— It was best not to think of those intimacies. He was hurting enough without adding fuel to the fire.

He reached for the phone and dialed Perry's number at the hotel. When he was put through, a very drowsy voice answered.

"Perry? Get moving and call Dubliss in Zurich and tell him we're postponing the Debuk project."

Perry's voice was suddenly wide awake. "You're not going after her?"

"I didn't say that. The project is still go—we're just handling it differently. I'm going in ahead tomorrow and I'll contact him with further instructions when I arrive."

"Am I going with you?"

"No, you'll join Dubliss day after tomorrow when you've finished tying up the loose ends here."

"Loose ends?" Perry asked warily.

"I want you to stall the merger negotiations."

"Cripes, why was I afraid that was what you meant?" he asked gloomily. "The AirFlow Board of Directors will tear me apart. I may not be able to make it to Zurich in one piece."

"You'll make it," Zack said. "Tell Dubliss to stay ready."

"Right. The same general plan as before?"

"We may have to make a few adjustments. I'll let you know. Good night, Perry."

"Fat chance," Perry said sourly. "I have a few dozen things to do before I beard the AirFlow

board. One of them is to build a fallout shelter."
The dial tone sounded as the connection was
broken.

Zack replaced the receiver and dropped into the
oversized desk chair. He should probably go to bed
and try to rest, even if he couldn't sleep. He'd been
on an exhaustive marathon lately with this merger
pending. He leaned back in the chair and closed
his eyes. He would go to bed soon. Now he wanted
to sit and think about Kira, to savor the way she
had looked, the responses she had made to him.
Then he would think about the *mondava*.

Three

The early morning sunlight was strong, with the sort of clarity found only in the high country. The softening mist had burned off, leaving the Santa Catalinas stark and brutally beautiful against the cerulean sky.

Kira breathed deeply, letting the piñon-scented breeze intoxicate her with its tangy fragrance. That same breeze lifted her hair away from her face in a gentle caress and tugged like a playful child at her yellow robe. Her hands tightened on the redwood railing of the balcony. No wonder Zack had built his lodge on the side of this mountain. The simplicity and power of the man were echoed in these surroundings.

She crossed her arms over her chest as a little shiver ran through her. She had been determined not to let Zack Damon intimidate her, but, apparently, in order to block out uncertainty it was necessary not to think at all. Which was going to be a near impossible task when even the blasted mountains reminded her of him.

She had been unable to sleep for a long time after she'd gone to bed. Her mind had been a turmoil of jumbled thoughts, impressions, and apprehensions. Why was she so upset? It wasn't like her to brood about things she couldn't help. There was a price to be paid and she would pay it. Zack Damon was both attractive physically and fascinating mentally. And, she went on thinking, there had to be scores of women who would do virtually anything to wind up in bed with him. It wasn't as if Kira had any hang-ups about her virginity, for heaven's sake. Stefan was the conservative one, not she. There just hadn't been a man who appealed to her in that way before.

And there was certainly no doubt that Zack did appeal to her sensually, she thought, amused that she'd used such a tepid word as "appeal" to describe how he made her feel. Her reaction to him had been near inflammatory in the brief time they'd been together. It wouldn't be any hardship giving him what he'd asked, if she could only get rid of this uncharacteristic shyness.

"Do you like my mountains?" Zack asked from behind her.

She whirled to face him. He leaned against the jamb of the sliding glass doors, watching her. He was dressed in jeans and a cream-colored sweatshirt, but the casual garb did nothing to diminish his aura of controlled power. If anything, it augmented it. Now he blended into his surroundings, rather than standing deliberately apart, and she again had the feeling he was drawing power from everything around him.

"I didn't mean to startle you. I brought your breakfast tray. I knocked, but you evidently didn't hear me."

"No." She felt suddenly tongue-tied as she gazed up at him. "I thought Juana was going to bring my tray. Do you usually provide personal service to your houseguests?"

"I wanted to see you," he said simply. "I couldn't sleep for thinking about you last night."

Her eyes widened. "Why?"

"You persist in questioning the obvious." He smiled, his eyes bright with amusement. "If I tell you, do you promise to blush again?"

"How unkind. I know it's provincial, but I can't help blushing. I assure you I'm working on eliminating it."

"Don't. I like your blushes. Every time I see the heat beneath your skin I want to reach out and touch you, feel the heat, the softness, the silk."

She tried, but couldn't manage, to look away from him. That maddening color rose to her cheeks. "Your words are very pretty, but I'd prefer to appear sophisticated rather than naive." Her lips were trembling as she smiled at him. "I'm not usually like this, you know. For some reason, you make me a bit nervous."

His smile faded. "I don't want that. I want you to feel entirely comfortable with me."

How could she when the mere sight of him caused her breath to catch in her throat and her legs to turn boneless? She glanced away. "I will. It will just take time. I've never met anyone like you before. I'm more accustomed to men who are social butterfly types than to men who are so serious about everything."

He frowned. "You think I lack a sense of humor?"

"No, you're just more . . . intense."

"Yes, I am intense. I don't believe you should do anything unless you're prepared to throw everything you have into it. But then, you should understand. You're an exceptionally intense person yourself."

Her gaze flew back to him. "Who me? You have the wrong lady. I'm known as the original scatterbrained madcap. Ask anyone."

"I don't need to ask anyone. I prefer to form my own judgments." His eyes narrowed on her face. "And I think you're probably one of the most intense people I've ever met. I wonder why you're so determined to hide that intensity?"

"I'm not hiding anything." She turned her back on him and stared at the mountains. "You asked me if I like your mountains. Do you own them?"

He walked to her side. "I own them. I don't have a deed to them, but they're still mine."

"What?" she asked, puzzled.

"My grandfather used to say that if you love something enough, you become one with it. One entity flows into the other to merge and then to seal." His gaze was fixed on the mountains with possessiveness as well as affection. "Yes, in spirit these mountains belong to me."

"That's rather an abstract philosophy for a tough businessman to have adopted. I would think your instincts would lead you to pin down anything you wanted, to buy it outright and to have the deed in your pocket."

"No one has just one face, particularly not me. There are times when I want to reach out and grab." His gaze was still fastened on the mountain peaks. "And there are other times when I think that the only way to keep what's mine is to let it go." He turned to face her, his gaze meeting her own with the same intensity with which he had regarded the mountains. "That's what many Indian tribes believed, you know. They would strive very hard to acquire rich trappings, slaves, and horses, only to give them away to show how little material wealth actually meant to them. It wasn't the acquisition but the release that was important." His tone was halting, as if he were trying to express something beyond the surface meaning of the words. "Do you understand what I'm saying to you?"

She shook her head. "I don't think so. It's clear you wouldn't be in the position you're in now if you gave everything away, so you must subscribe to a more materialistic philosophy than your grandfather's."

He was silent for a moment and then he smiled cynically. "You're right, of course. I'm probably far more philistine than shaman. I suppose I wanted to justify myself in your eyes. I don't know why. I've never been tempted to do that before." He turned away abruptly. "Come along inside and have your breakfast. The plane will be ready in two hours."

She was troubled as she trailed him into the room, pausing beside the bed on which he had deposited the wicker breakfast tray. She had the vague impression that she had hurt him in some way, and it was causing an odd aching deep inside her. "I may not understand you, but I'm not stupid enough to think I have any right to judge an unknown quantity," she said gently. "Marna trusts you, so I'm sure you can't be as ruthless as you've been portrayed."

"But I am ruthless," he said softly. "It's the other side of the coin. Not with you, though, Kira. You won't ever have to worry about seeing the ruthlessness in me."

His expression was enigmatic, yet it once again generated within her the warm languid heat she had known last night. She drew a deep, shaky breath and tried to smile. "I'll be very grateful for that. I don't think I'm equipped to handle a man like you, Zack."

There was a sudden glint of mischief in his eyes. "It's a skill I expect to enjoy teaching you. It will be an exquisite pleasure being handled by you." He held out his hand. "Starting now. Come here, Kira."

She hesitated. "You said we had to leave soon," she murmured.

"Not that soon." He smiled with a warmth that bemused her. Such a lovely smile, full of gentleness and understanding and . . . "Come to me."

Her gaze clung to his as she moved slowly toward him. There was something there, waiting just beyond his glowing intensity. She came to a halt before him and looked up at him searchingly. It was still there, still waiting. She had always hated waiting, she thought hazily, and this waiting was centuries old and curiously timeless.

His hand was waiting for her, too, outstretched in silent invitation. She slipped her small hand into his large one with the supreme naturalness of a trusting child and suddenly experienced a tingling shock of sensation that was immediately drowned in a sparkling sense of perfect *rightness*. "Hello," she whispered.

"Hello," he said thickly. "Welcome home, love."

Home. Yes, that's what was waiting for her. Why hadn't she realized it? What had been before, was happening again. A smile suddenly lit her face with radiance. "Oh, I'm so happy. I do love—" She broke off. There was something wrong. She frowned, trying to pierce the mists obscuring the shining truth she'd known just a minute before. "Zack?"

His smile was fading as his hand tightened around her own. "I'm still here, Kira. I'll always be here."

"Yes, I know, but there's something wrong. Something—" She stopped again. Then she shook her head as if to clear it. Crazy. What had happened was completely crazy. Her nerves must be more strained than she thought to have tricked her into a wild flight of fancy. She closed her eyes for an instant and drew a deep, steadying breath. She was experiencing a poignant disappointment that was shaking her to the core and was as insane as the rest of it. She didn't want to return to reality when that moment of piercing recognition had been so magnificent. Recognition? Oh, Lord, she *was* going mad. Her eyes opened and she smiled with forced gaiety. "Sorry. I think you must have mesmerized me for a moment. Are you sure you're not a shaman too?"

There was a flicker in his eyes that might have reflected the same wild disappointment she was feeling. "I'm sure."

"Well, you could have fooled me," she said flippantly. "Do you get that response from Mallory Thane too?"

"No."

Kira could feel the wild color sting her cheeks. She was suddenly feverish. "I'm surprised." Her tongue moistened her lower lip. "I hear you're quite the ladies' man and she's known to be—"

"Be quiet." His voice was very soft to be so commanding. "I know you're frightened, but stop trying to put barriers between us." He released her hand and suddenly was cupping her shoulders. He shook her gently. "Mallory Thane isn't important. None of them were important, and now they're all simply past history."

She wouldn't look at him. Her gaze was fastened stubbornly on the middle of his chest. "You were expecting her here last night."

"No, I wasn't expecting anyone but you."

She believed him, and that was as crazy and frightening as everything else that had gone before. "I don't understand any of this."

"You will." His hands moved from her shoulders gently to cup her face in his palms. "It isn't time yet. Trust me, Kira."

"I'm trying." Her words were a mere whisper. "I have to trust someone. I don't seem to have much confidence in myself anymore."

"Do you suppose you could stretch that faith

enough to look up at me?" There was a thread of gentle humor in his voice. "I think your fierce glare is burning a hole through my breastbone."

Her gaze lifted, and his look of tenderness and understanding was like a soothing balm to her troubled spirit.

"That's better." He smiled. "For a moment I thought we'd skipped a few hurdles, but evidently it wasn't meant to be." His thumbs splayed out across her cheekbones to rub gently at the corners of her lips. "Perhaps it's better this way. We have so much to experience, and everything is bright and shining and new." His head came down slowly. "I'm going to kiss you. Is that all right with you, love?"

He was only a breath away, his dark eyes holding her own. She could feel the warmth radiating from his body and smell the clean, fresh scent of him. Her throat was so tight the assent came out a little huskily. "Yes."

She had expected warmth and gentleness, but not the honey sweetness. His lips were hard and firm, yet they wooed and tempted, cherished and promised. He built labyrinths of golden intimacy and then led her through them so lovingly she thought her heart would stop with each new, exquisite twist and turn. She didn't know how many times their lips met and parted or how many ways his hands moved and angled her head to take and give and take again. Time flowed, intimacy deepened. Time flowed again. Such a beautiful, meaningful circle, she thought dreamily.

His head lifted at last and he looked down at her.

His eyes were night-black, the pupils dilated. "Good?" he asked softly.

"Wonderful . . ." She wished he hadn't stopped. Her lips felt soft, pliant; she ached for the sweetness of his lips, and the pain was almost as sharp as the desire she'd known last night. How strange and wonderful were the heights to which his mere kiss could lift her. "I wish it could go on forever."

"It can't, though." His lips were pressing soft, loving kisses on her cheeks, the tip of her nose, her temple. "There's too much electricity stored up between us." He tilted her head back and his warm lips drifted over the sensitive cord of her throat. "It has to change, but we'll always have this to come back to, you know."

"Will we?" It was very comforting to know that, she thought hazily. But he was right; it was already changing. His lips were growing hotter against her throat and she could see his chest rising and falling with the harshness of his breathing. The tiny changes she could detect in his body triggered identical ones within her own. She was no longer languid and dreamy.

The sensations she was feeling now were all sharp and aching and fever-hot, and she wasn't sure she wanted to be jarred out of blissful euphoria. There was a liquid throbbing between her thighs and her breasts felt full and painfully swollen. She wished he'd move his hands from her face and put them on her breasts. Perhaps that caress would ease their strange aching. She was vaguely surprised that the desire didn't shock her. She had never before wanted a man's hands on her, touching intimately. Yet she supposed it shouldn't have surprised her. There was no comparing any of the emotions she was feeling for Zack with those in her previous experience.

The muscles of his body were hardening, rippling. She was aware of that meaningful tautening, even though he was only touching her with his hands. His body was readying itself. The knowledge sent a near savage jolt of pure desire through her. He wanted her. She could see the pulse leaping crazily in his temple and feel the soft nip of his teeth on the flesh of her throat.

"You see?" His voice was guttural. He lifted his head and his face was flushed and heavy with sensuality. "It never stays the same. There's too much waiting for us."

"Yes," she whispered. She wondered if her eyes were as glazed and wanting as his. They probably were. She felt as if every breath she drew was exploding little fiery sparks into her bloodstream.

"I want to touch you. I want my hands on you."

"Yes," she said again. She couldn't seem to say anything else to him. Response and assent. The reaction was as basic as nature itself.

"You want it too? I don't want to take, Kira."

"I want it too."

His lips curved in a rare smile. "That's all I wanted to know. I'm surprised I even had the restraint to look this particular gift horse in the mouth. Come along, love."

He was taking her by the hand and, to her surprise, leading her away from the bed across the room. "Where are we going?"

"Right here." He had stopped beside the deep-cushioned contemporary easy chair against the wall. He sat down and positioned her between his legs. "If we used the bed, I'm sure this preliminary foray would result in an instant merger." His hands were swiftly untying the belt of her robe.

She felt a swift thrust of disappointment. "I assumed you had grown impatient with your little anticipatory game."

"I am impatient," he said dryly. "And hurting and . . ." He opened the robe and stared at her for a long moment. She felt scorched, burned, and knew her body was responding helplessly and very obviously to his hot, lingering appraisal. The sheer veiling of the yellow chiffon nightgown might just as well not have been there for all the covering it gave her. "Oh, Lord, am I hurting."

And so was she. The robe dropped, making a pool of sunshine color on the dark brown carpet at her feet, and she stood before him in only the sheer nightgown. There was something vaguely barbaric about their positions—Zack sitting fully clothed and she standing almost naked between his legs like a slave girl waiting to pleasure him.

"What are you thinking about?" His gaze had moved from her body to her face. The tip of his tongue reached out to moisten his lower lip and the unconscious motion sent a surge of aching tension to every muscle in her body. Sweet heaven, those lips were so diabolically and beautifully sensual in his taut face.

"I think you know."

"I probably have a good idea." His gaze traveled slowly from the creamy satin of her shoulders to the full thrust of her breasts against the chiffon. "Do you like me to look at you?"

"Yes."

"That's good. I think there's every chance it will be one of my very favorite things to do." He slowly reached up and slid first one thin strap off her shoulder, then the other. The bodice of the gown slipped until only the swollen fullness of her breasts was holding the clinging material in place. Zack leaned back in the chair and simply looked at her for a long moment. "You have wonderful skin. It radiates a sheen that glows with life."

"Do I?" She scarcely knew what she was saying. How could he just sit there looking at her when every muscle and nerve in her body was on fire with frustration? Why didn't he *touch* her?

"Yes." He leaned forward and laid his cheek against her abdomen. She inhaled sharply as she felt the sudden warmth of his flesh through the sheer fabric of the nightgown. "Wonderful skin. Strong, firm muscles." One big hand was lazily rubbing her belly. "And softness." His palm slid down to gently cup the apex of her thighs so that only the mist of material separated him from that most intimate part of her. She could feel the heat of his hard hand and made a low sound deep in her throat as he started to rub back and forth, alternating hard pressure with gossamer lightness so that she could become accustomed to neither, his every touch then giving her a fresh jolt of sensation. "Do you like this?"

She nodded. She didn't think she could have spoken if her life had depended upon it. With his cheek pressed against her, he couldn't see the nod, but it didn't really matter. He knew very well what pleasure he was giving her. "What else would you like me to do to you?"

She could scarcely breathe. How could he expect her to speak? But he evidently did, for he was lifting his head to look up at her. His hand was still moving gently against her. "What else, Kira?"

Her tongue moistened her dry lips. "Zack . . ." Her gaze dropped helplessly to the sheer chiffon veiling her breasts. Her nipples were so exquisitely sensitive now that even the light wreath of material was causing them to ache.

His eyes followed hers and then grew midnight dark as he saw the hard, pointed tips thrusting at the material. "Your breasts?" His hand instantly reached out and hovered over her right breast. She could feel the warmth, though he wasn't touching her. "So swollen," he whispered, his eyes on the firm globes rising from the chiffon. "So ripe and swollen and ready." His hand closed suddenly over her breast and a wild shudder ran through her. "Ready for me."

"Yes. Oh, yes." The cry was wrung from her. "Please, please *do* something!"

"Shh, I will." He pulled her onto his lap, settling her astride him. His fingers were trembling as he pushed the chiffon the last few inches and bared her breasts. "Beautiful," he murmured. "Sweet heaven, you're beautiful, Kira." He lowered his head slowly. She felt his warm breath, then the firmness of his lips, and she gave a low, frantic half-moan, her fingers tangling in his hair, bringing him to her.

Kira heard his low laugh. Strangely, it held no hint of triumph, only an exultant joy. "You *want* me. Lord, I love to know that." The words were muffled against her breast. Then his mouth was opening, taking her, his tongue running over one breast in wild delight and then switching to her other breast to suckle and pleasure her with a hunger that soothed even as it inflamed.

She was vaguely aware of his hands on her thighs pushing up the chiffon while his lips and teeth nibbled, nipped, and then soothed with a deep, primitive enjoyment. His chest was shuddering with every breath and his hands were suddenly frantic as they slipped under the gown and cupped her naked buttocks in his warm palms. Another shock, she thought hazily. Every different touch was a fresh shock to her nerve endings, but a shock that she accepted happily and with amazing rapidity. He was pressing her closer and she felt his iron-hard warmth against the center of her womanhood. She nestled even closer and moaned with hunger. Hunger. She had never known such hunger. He kept taking, giving, but it made no difference. The hunger kept growing, sharpening with every passing moment.

"We have to stop, you know," he muttered. His hands tightened on her flesh as if to refute his words. "Kira . . ."

"No!" He couldn't stop now. The hunger was so intense it was hurting her. Was this what he meant when he said that he was hurting? Her hands gentled his hair as she felt a rush of almost maternal feeling. "Please. Don't stop."

"Do you think I want to?" he growled. His eyes closed. "It's out of control. I didn't expect you to be this . . . loving."

Loving. The word should have been out of place, but somehow it wasn't. Lust alone could never be this emotionally intense—there had to be a strong element of love in it. Her fingers ran through his hair yearningly, adoring the crisp texture between her fingers. "That's the way I feel," she said softly. "I want . . ." Her voice trailed off. There was so much she wanted all at once that she suddenly felt as though she'd been catapulted into a strange emotional maze. Assuagement on a physical level alone wouldn't be enough, yet what else could she hope for? Zack was a stranger.

"So do I," he said huskily. His eyes opened to reveal unbearable strain. "But we can't have it. Not yet." He was swiftly shifting her off him and standing up. "It has to be right."

"Right?" He was *leaving* her. She couldn't keep the note of disbelief and frustration out of her voice as she watched him stride swiftly toward the door. "Isn't it a little late to worry about—" She cut the words off abruptly. Her fingers automatically went to her bodice and pulled up the straps of the gown. "I don't understand any of this. Why did you do this to us if you weren't going to finish what you started?"

He turned at the door, his face taut with pain. "I know you don't understand. I told you, I miscalculated. I thought I could take a little and lessen this damn hunger I have for you. But it didn't work out that way. It only made it worse." His gaze traveled over her and she felt as if he were touching her again. "I'm not even going to be able to look at you or touch your hand without wanting this again."

"Why?" she asked. Her hands tightened on the

arms of the chair. "What's the difference whether it's now or later."

"You have the right to *know* me," he said harshly. "I may not be able to hold out for very long, but I don't want to be a faceless stranger to you when I first make love to you. I want it to be right, dammit. If I didn't think it was important, do you believe I would have let you go?" He drew a deep, shuddering breath. "You'd better get dressed. We'll be leaving for Tamrovia within the hour."

He closed the door with quiet restraint and it seemed more explosive than a slam to Kira.

She gazed blankly at the door for a moment before she could even consider moving from the chair. She had a vague feeling she should be resentful toward Zack for having wrested the decision from her so summarily. Yet how could she regret the fact that he had been willing to undergo such painful self-denial in order to spare her the possibility of feeling cheapened?

He wanted her to have a chance to get to know him, but in a strange, incomprehensible way she felt that getting to know him was completely unnecessary. She did know him. She knew he was honest and had a code of ethics that would be even harder on him than on those around him. She knew that his loyalty, once given, would be as unshakable as those mountains he had claimed as his own. The knowledge was so fundamentally instinctive she didn't even question it.

Something was happening to them, and although she was still bewildered, she was no longer frightened. Instead, she was beginning to experience a buoyant exhilaration like nothing she had ever known before. It was as if a wonderfully thrilling adventure were hovering on the horizon and all she had to do was move toward it and it would be *hers*. Dear Lord, how she wanted that adventure!

She jumped up and bent to retrieve the yellow silk robe on the floor. She had to shower, dress, and then repack her night things. She cast a glance at the covered tray on the bed and made a face. The food was probably stone-cold by now. Even if it was still edible, she was too emotion-charged to find food appetizing at the moment. Perhaps she would be able to eat something later on the plane.

Her steps were quick and light, with just a hint of ebullience, as she crossed the carpet toward the adjoining bathroom.

"You seem to be in a good mood," Zack said, his eyes narrowed on her face. "I had no idea you'd be this happy to get back to Tamrovia. Somehow I got the impression you weren't overly fond of your native land."

"I'm not. Oh, that's not true. I guess I actually love it." Kira slipped her arms into the pearl-gray suit jacket she'd removed for the trip. "It's just that I always feel a sense of oppression when I step off a plane onto Tamrovian soil." She wrinkled her nose. "Which doesn't indicate that I'm particularly sensitive. Stefan is known to have the same effect on the entire country. No one has ever told him monarchs can't censor the press and outlaw trade unions in this century. Or, if they have, he hasn't really heard it."

"And no habeas corpus," Zack said thoughtfully. "His particular form of deafness could be very dangerous."

"Why do you think Stefan has tightened the exit visa restrictions and strengthened the complement of border guards? The Tamrovian factories are all pitifully undermanned because workers are leaving Tamrovia for Germany and Switzerland. Who can blame them?"

A curious smile touched Zack's face. "You seem very well informed for a 'scatterbrained madcap.' "

Her glance slid away from his. "It's common knowledge. I just don't bury my head in the sand the way Stefan does."

"Perhaps." He unfastened his seat belt as the Lear Jet came to a rolling stop before a hangar in the private sector of the airport. "You didn't answer my question. Why are you in such good spirits all of a sudden?"

She still didn't look at him. "Why shouldn't I be happy? You've promised to free Marna and that's very important to me."

His hand reached out and fastened on her arm. She could feel the warmth and strength of it through the linen blazer. His eyes met hers with searching gravity. "No games. Truth."

She opened her lips to make another evasive answer and then closed them again. She didn't want to evade him, even if it meant exposing her vulnerability. "I don't know," she said simply. "I'm just happy. I think it has something to do with you, Zack."

His hand tightened on her arm for the briefest instant. "Dear Lord, I hope so." Then his hand was releasing her and he was rising to his feet. "Come on. Let's get this show on the road. The sooner we can get Marna out, the sooner we can move on to more important things."

She raised an inquiring brow. "For instance?"

His eyes twinkled. "Why, the *mondava*, of course."

She cast him an exasperated glance. "Now who's playing games? If you won't let me in on the big secret, it's not very kind of you to tease me with it."

"Sorry, you're right. I'm not being fair." His voice lowered to velvet softness. "I think I went a little giddy for a moment. You see, I find I'm very happy too. Strange, isn't it?"

She was having trouble tearing her gaze away from his. She was sure his eyes spoke of many fascinating things if only she could understand. She stood and picked up her handbag. "We haven't decided what story we're going to tell Stefan about our relationship. Hadn't we better put our heads together?"

"Not exactly the portions of our anatomies I was interested in joining," he murmured. "But if you insist . . ." His brow gathered in a thoughtful frown. "Where were you six months ago?"

"Sedikhan."

"Then that's where we met. I was really in seclusion in Switzerland, putting together a pharmaceutical combine, but only a few people know that. It wouldn't have been unheard of for me to fly to Marasef for a conference with Alex Ben Raschid and run into you there. I took one look at you and—*voilà*—instant passion."

She frowned. "I'm not the kind of woman who inspires instant insanity in men, Zack. Do you think anyone will believe it?"

He slowly shook his head. "What am I going to do with you? In case you didn't notice, only this morning I gave an extemporaneous demonstration of how insane you're capable of driving a man." His finger gently touched the hollow of her cheek. "I promise to be very convincing. Okay?"

"Okay," she said softly. Happiness bubbled up in her like a clear, golden stream. She turned away as the door of the Lear Jet opened and stairs were rolled up to the entrance. "If you don't think Stefan will think something is fishy."

"Let me take care of it. I've probably handled more difficult customers than your brother Stefan. Corporate types are far more ruthless than diplomats."

"I just might do that. I haven't had any great degree of luck in influencing Stefan up to the present."

"I've noticed," he said dryly as he took her elbow and urged her toward the door. "I'm surprised that Marna didn't just put a spell on him instead of your unfortunate suitors."

"She couldn't. It would have been a gesture of disloyalty to the royal household and would have broken the tradition that binds her people to the Rubinoff dynasty." She suddenly frowned as her gaze swept over his big body, still garbed in the sweatshirt and jeans he'd put on that morning. "Where is your jacket?"

His eyes widened in surprise. "What?"

"You can't go outside like that."

He went still. "Is Her Highness ashamed to be seen with me?"

"Don't be stupid," she said crossly. "It may be hot in Tucson, but it's autumn in the Balkans, and it can be very cool here in October. You can't run around just in jeans and a sweatshirt. You might catch cold."

"Really." A flicker of tenderness transformed the wary hardness of his face. "Well, I certainly wouldn't want to do that. A cold in the head might prove very inconvenient at the moment." He opened a shallow closet, pulled out a beige suede jacket, and slipped it on. "Satisfied?"

She nodded contentedly. "Yes. Now you're being sensible."

"I'm known to be a very sensible man." He directed a grin at her before he stepped back to allow her to precede him down the stairs. "Sometimes."

"Your dual personality?" she asked over her shoulder. "I would think you'd feel very Jekyll and Hyde with—"

"Who's that?" Zack's gaze had focused on someone beyond her shoulder and his voice was so sharp it startled her.

Her head turned to follow his gaze and she unconsciously tensed. "We're evidently about to be honored," she said quietly as she watched the tall, lean man approaching them with leisurely catlike grace. "It's Sandor Karpathan."

Zack gave a low whistle. "This little junket may

prove more entertaining than I thought. I can see why he made you uneasy. He has—"

"*Condar.* Strength," Kira finished flatly. "Marna says he is a *disek*, one of the exceptional ones who can be anything he wants to be. But *diseks* can be evil as well as good. She doesn't trust him. She says there is something not as it should be."

Condar. Yes, the word suited Karpathan, just as the impression inherent in the word *power* fitted Zack. He was in his middle thirties and his slender body was clothed in a flawlessly tailored three-piece beige suit, which he wore with effortless grace. His hair was dark and barbered by a master hand, his shoes shined to a mirror gloss. His features were just as perfect as his dress and he should have looked a trifle effeminate. But there was nothing effeminate about Sandor Karpathan. He appeared to be tough, intelligent, and dangerous.

His smile was a brilliant flash in his bronzed face as he stopped before her and bowed. "Your Highness, I was informed by immigration that you would be arriving this afternoon and I took this opportunity to come and meet you."

"How kind of you, Sandor," Kira said ironically. "I didn't realize you'd missed me. I've only been gone three days."

"But we always miss you, no matter how short your journey," he said softly. "There are some people who take the sunshine with them when they leave."

"How very flowery. I'm sure both you and Tamrovia survived my absence." Karpathan and Zack were sizing each other up like two gladiators about to enter the arena, and she doubted if either man heard her. "However, I think it far more likely you were interested in the information immigration gave you regarding my companion."

Karpathan shrugged. "I admit to a touch of curiosity. After all. I'm only human." His smile was totally charming. "The two of you made every newspaper in Europe this morning. Mr. Damon is such an elusive man; I found it very interesting that you managed to capture him."

"But she didn't." Zack took a step closer and his arm slid around her waist in swift possession. "I'm the one who captured her. Introduce us, Kira."

"Of course," she said quickly. "Zack Damon, this is His Grace, Sandor Anton Karpathan, the Duke of Limtana and personal adviser to my brother."

Karpathan held out his hand. "My friends at Oxford called me Sand." He grinned. "I think it was meant to remind me that the title didn't give me any right to put on airs. I hope you will call me Sand."

Zack took his hand and found himself looking into eyes of deep sapphire-blue. Very familiar eyes. He glanced at Kira. "You're related?"

"The eyes?" She nodded. "We're distant cousins. That particular color seems to pop up repeatedly in the family."

Karpathan grimaced. "You notice the emphasis on distant? I can't seem to convince Kira what a wonderful fellow I am. I hope you'll be more ready to accept my friendship."

"Why do you want to be friends with me?" Zack asked bluntly. "I'm here purely for a social visit because Kira wanted me to see her country."

"How very sentimental," Karpathan murmured.
"Kira must have a very odd effect on you. I hadn't
heard that you were prone to such emotion."

"She does have an odd effect on me," Zack said
quietly. "But I'm enjoying the hell out of it."

There was an elusive flicker in Karpathan's eyes.
"I believe you're sincere. How refreshing. I'm afraid
I've become something of a cynic. and I admit I
doubted your devotion to my little cousin."

"I'm very devoted." Zack smiled gently. "Why
shouldn't I be? You said yourself that Kira walks in
sunshine."

"Not you too," Kira wailed, wrinkling her nose.
"I'm beginning to get a little nauseous with all this
sweet talk floating around."

"You're right. She's very hard to convince."
Zack's gaze met Karpathan's. "That's why I'm here.
When we met six months ago in Sedikhan, I told
her we were meant for each other, but she thought
I was crazy. I've got to convince her that I'm not a
man to change his mind."

"I don't think there's any doubt about it,"
Karpathan said lightly. "When we heard you were
coming, Stefan and I hoped we could interest you
in investing in a few industries that need a little
shoring up. We're obviously going to be disappointed." He shrugged. "Oh, well, perhaps we can
still lure you into our toils. Stefan is giving a reception in your honor tomorrow night at the palace.
I'll invite a few key men to whom you might be
interested in talking. Now, may I offer you a ride to
the palace? Stefan is very eager to meet you."

"I just bet he is," Kira muttered.

Karpathan gave her an amused glance. "You can

hardly blame him. It's not every day that Zack Damon is brought into the fold. You must admit you've proved very difficult in the past, Kira. Stefan is delighted that you've finally managed to get it right."

Kira opened her lips to speak, but Zack quickly said, "We don't need a lift." He nodded toward the dark brown Mercedes parked by the high wire fence bordering the runway. "I arranged to have one of my people meet us."

"Oh, yes. I forgot you have contacts everywhere. Even in our small and unimportant country." He inclined his head. "Then I'll see you at the palace." He turned and walked swiftly in the direction of the navy-blue limousine parked to the left of the hangar.

Zack was silent as he escorted Kira across the tarmac to the Mercedes. He greeted the driver briefly and helped her into the backseat of the car. Then he settled back against the cushioned upholstery with an absent frown on his face. The car started and began to move out of the airport parking lot with an almost soundless hum of motion.

Kira turned to face him. "Well?"

He looked at her inquiringly.

"Karpathan," she said with a touch of impatience. "What do you think?"

"I think both you and Marna are right," he said quietly. "He is a *disek*. As for what else he is, I have no idea. I'll have to find out." He reached out and laced his fingers through hers. It was a companionable, intimate gesture, and a tiny river of warmth flowed through her. "And I think we're definitely going to have an interesting few days in picturesque Tamrovia."

Four

"Stefan appears to be an amazingly lax guardian of your morals," Zack said from the doorway of his adjoining suite. "He didn't even pretend to want to save you from my clutches."

Kira took off her suit jacket and tossed it on the couch. "If he hadn't thought I was willing to sleep with you, he'd probably have put you in here with me and seen that the door was locked every night."

Zack lifted a brow. "Surely you're exaggerating."

"Perhaps a little," she said wearily as she kicked off her high heels. "But you saw how Stefan fawned all over you when you were introduced. My clever cousin was correct. It seems that at last I've done something right in Stefan's eyes. Maybe I should have turned whore for the glory of Tamrovia and Stefan before this. It might have been easier than fighting his plans for an arranged marriage."

The amusement left Zack's face. "I guarantee it wouldn't have been easy at all," he said with dangerous softness. "And totally impossible now that you've agreed to belong to me."

Her eyes widened in surprise. "I was joking, for heaven's sake."

"There are some subjects I don't find funny. You just happen to have hit on the one at the top of the list." He was silent for a moment, his gaze on her face. "And I don't think you find the idea amusing either. What's wrong, Kira?"

She laughed shortly. "Why, nothing at all. What could possibly be wrong? Shouldn't I be thrilled to have spent the last hour with the three of you treating me as if I were a prize poodle to be petted and taught new tricks? I'm a *person*, dammit!"

"I know that," he said quietly. "I thought you realized I'd have to behave with you as I ordinarily would with a mistress."

She felt a swift jab of pain. "You did it very well. You would, of course, considering your experience. How many women have you—" She broke off. "I'm sorry. So sorry. I don't have any right to ask you such a question. And I know you had to act as you did in the throne room." She met his gaze fiercely. "But Stefan didn't and neither did Sandor. I felt . . . valueless."

"I have an idea Karpathan was following Stefan's lead," he said thoughtfully. "Giving an inch so he could take a mile at some other point along the road. I'm sorry I didn't cut the meeting short when I saw the way it was going, but I wanted to observe Karpathan with your brother." He smiled faintly. "It was very enlightening."

"Enlightening?"

"Karpathan is very clever. The strings are almost invisible and Stefan is completely unaware he's dancing on them."

"You think Stefan is being manipulated?"

Zack nodded. "I'd say Stefan hasn't made a move that wasn't in accordance with Karpathan's wishes since your cousin became his adviser."

Kira shivered. "I thought so. Which is going to make it much more difficult to get Marna out of Tamrovia, isn't it?"

"Possibly." Then, as he saw her troubled frown, he added gently, "But we'll do it anyway. I promised you, Kira."

She could feel power and reassurance flow out to her and her expression gradually cleared. "I know you did, and I'm definitely going to hold you to it," she said lightly. "Do you have any ideas as to how we're going to manage it?"

"A few," he said absently. His gaze traveled past her to the photograph on the wall across the room. "Is that one of yours?"

She turned to the black-and-white blowup he was indicating. "Yes," she said carelessly. She gestured to the opposite wall where there were a half dozen framed black-and-white photographs. "They're all mine. Photography is one of my hobbies."

"Yes, I know." He crossed the room and stood before the photograph that had caught his attention. "This is magnificent. You can almost feel the rage and frustration the man is feeling."

"Stefan thought so too," Kira said with a touch of grimness. "The original photograph appeared in the Belajo Sentinel. That's Marc Naldona, the trade union leader. I took it at a secret torchlight meeting in the woods north of the city a little over a year ago. Stefan was perfectly furious. He confiscated my camera and lectured me for two days." She regarded the photograph somberly. "He also exiled the editor of the newspaper and installed one of his stooges in his place. Then Stefan tried to arrest Naldona, but he was warned and fled the city before the soldiers arrived."

"Don't look now, but I think your madcap facade is slipping drastically," Zack said softly. "Do I detect a note of patriotism?"

She shook her head. "I tried to do something when I realized how bad Stefan was for Tamrovia, but he made quite sure I was helpless. I was a doll to be manipulated. That was why I chose to spend my school years in America and my vacations in Sedikhan. I don't *want* to care when I have no power to change what's happening here."

"But you do care."

She smiled a little sadly. "Then I'll have to get over it, won't I? Because if I manage to get Marna out of Tamrovia this time, I don't think I'll be able to come back. Karpathan will make quite sure that Stefan refuses to let me return." She straightened her shoulders with a touch of bravado and lifted her chin. "It looks as if I'll have to consider a career. Do you think I could make a living as a photographer?"

"Yes, if that's what you want. I think you can be anything you want to be," Zack said gently. "These photographs are brilliant. Did you take them with the Nikon?"

"Yes, I used a long-range—" She stared at him. "How did you know I had a Nikon?"

"I must have read it somewhere." His eyes were still on the photograph.

She frowned. "I didn't think any of the reporters knew about my work. It's not something I talk about."

"How else could I have known?"

She shrugged wearily. "I guess you couldn't. Lord, there's no way to keep anything private these days, is there?"

"Was it the Nikon your brother took away from you?"

"Yes, it nearly broke my heart. I loved that camera. Marna gave it to me for my eighteenth birthday and it was absolutely wonderful. It must have cost her a small fortune. I felt guilty accepting it from her, but I couldn't resist." She made a face. "Stefan wasn't about to let me have anything that might stimulate my independence and take my mind off what he considered my duty."

"You made good use of the camera while you had it. These photographs are exceptional. I'll buy you another one as soon as we return to the States."

"No," she said emphatically. "I'll buy it myself and this time I won't let anyone take it away from me."

There was a little flicker of pride in his dark eyes. "No, I don't think you will." He turned away from the photograph. "We'll discuss it once we're out of Tamrovia. I believe we'd better accomplish that as soon as possible, considering Karpathan is here."

She became very still. "When?"

"I think tomorrow night during the reception

will be as good a time as any. From what he said, Stefan appears to be inviting practically the entire business and social world of Tamrovia to the festivities. It should be relatively easy to smuggle Marna out of the palace during the party."

"Tomorrow?" Kira felt a frisson of nervousness, but she suppressed it immediately. He was right, the sooner the better. "Easy? There are two guards in front of her door at all times."

"Guards can be bribed and palace guards aren't nearly as uncorruptible as your brother would like to think."

"A bribe takes time," Kira said skeptically. "The last time we broke her out of prison it took three weeks for Clancy and me to find a susceptible guard and persuade him it would be safe to take a bribe. You're only allowing yourself a little over twenty-four hours."

"I'll manage." He didn't look at her as he shrugged out of his suede jacket and tossed it next to her suit jacket on the couch. "Trust me."

"You seem to be saying that quite a bit lately," she said with a sigh. "I don't have a great deal of choice, do I?"

"You won't be sorry." He smiled. "Now I think you had better put on your shoes again and take me to see Marna. It would be a good idea to let her know what's in the wind so she can be prepared."

"I thought we'd go later and have dinner with her."

He shook his head. Karpathan and Stefan will assume we'll want to have dinner alone. We're lovers, remember?"

How could she forget? All he had to do was look

at her and she remembered how his mouth had felt on her . . . "All right," she said quickly as she walked to where she'd kicked off her high-heeled shoes beside the couch. "I'd forgotten." She slipped them on and gave her hair a cursory pat. "I'm ready."

"Not quite." He walked toward her. "We've been alone in this suite for almost an hour, and we're supposed to be unable to keep our hands off each other. You look much too proper."

She didn't feel at all proper. Her heart was beating so fast she expected it to leap out of her breast at any moment. "Really?"

He nodded slowly. "Really. Since we're going to be on public display, we should opt for authenticity." He took her in his arms. She hadn't thought her heart could race any faster, but she was wrong. "I told you I didn't like to do anything unless I could concentrate my entire attention on it," he said. His fingers tangled in her hair and he gently tugged her head back. "Open your mouth, love."

His tongue moved very delicately at first, slowly exploring the smoothness of her teeth and the dark cavity of her inner cheek, toying teasingly with her tongue. Then, with a sound that was a half-growl deep in his throat, the delicacy was gone. His tongue was spear-hard and his hands were hot and restless, running up and down her spine as if he couldn't touch enough of her.

A low, keening cry trembled in her throat as she arched into his body, her mouth opening wider to take more of him. His tongue was moving rhythmically, hotly, and his hands slid down to cup her buttocks and lift her into the hollow of his hips.

Arousal. Stark, hungry, shocking. She gasped and pressed herself closer with a little incoherent murmur.

Then, suddenly, Zack was stepping back, his chest moving heavily with the harshness of his breathing. He looked down at her flushed cheeks and bruised lips. "That's better," he said thickly. "But not quite good enough."

"No?" she asked dazedly.

His hands were quickly unbuttoning the pearl buttons of her silk blouse and drawing the material away from her breasts. He unfastened the front opening of her bra. "Stand still, love. It will only be a moment."

Then his mouth was enveloping her nipple and suckling gently. His hand framed the swollen mound, pumping rhythmically as his teeth pulled and his tongue soothed.

Stand still, he had told her. She couldn't have moved if she had tried. She couldn't do anything but look down at his dark head bent over her breast and watch as his lips and tongue moved on her flesh and drove her to the edge of insanity. Her breasts were lifting and falling as if she were running and she had to open her mouth wide to get air to her oxygen-starved lungs. Every pulling tug, every teasing brush of his tongue seemed to be connected to a burning wire which led to the apex of her thighs.

Then his head was lifting, his eyes, dark and wild and brilliant, staring into her own. "I think that should do it." His voice was hoarse and strained. "If I look like you do, there won't be any doubt about what we've been doing." His hands were trembling slightly as he fastened her bra and then buttoned her blouse. "Come on. Let's get out of here or we'll never get to see Marna today." His hand was beneath her elbow, propelling her toward the door.

Her knees felt like warm butter and she wasn't sure they'd support her. "Your methods are a little drastic. Was all that really necessary?"

He opened the door. "No, the kiss alone probably would have been sufficient to create the effect we needed for our audience." His eyes dropped compulsively to her full breasts pushing against the silk blouse. They were still swollen and taut and became even more so under his burning appraisal. "The rest was for me. I wanted to see you. I was hungry again. I think I'll always be hungry now. When we were in the throne room, all I could think of was how much I needed to have you on my lap as you were this morning, half-naked and wanting me, making those soft little sounds that—" He broke off, took a deep breath, and then let it out very slowly. "Later." Then he closed the door behind them and nudged her gently forward into the highly polished oak hallway. "I think it would be a good idea if you led the way, Kira. I appear to have lost my sense of direction at the moment."

The two armed guards standing before the double doors of Marna's suite were garbed in the elaborate dark blue dress uniforms of the Tamrovian army and reminded Zack vaguely of stage extras he'd seen in an operetta he'd attended in Paris.

They failed to challenge Kira as she opened the door and gave Zack no more than a passing glance.

"Not exactly razor-sharp security," Zack murmured to Kira as he followed her into the elegant suite and closed the door. "This may be easier than I thought."

"Stefan lets me come and go as I please," Kira said. "And everyone in the palace will have been told about you by now." The door opposite the sitting room opened and she was suddenly running toward the tall woman dressed in black who stood quietly in the doorway. "Marna!"

Kira was immediately folded in the woman's strong arms, her diminutive frame appearing even slighter in contrast with Marna Debuk's massive build. Zack hadn't remembered her as being that tall. The Gypsy towered over six feet and vaguely resembled a lady wrestler. The features of her face were harsh and blunt and her dark, shining hair was clubbed just below her ears. That impassive face didn't look any different from the way he remembered it over fifteen years ago. Her black eyes were just as snapping bright, her face as inscrutable and ageless as the day he'd first seen her when he was a boy of nineteen.

Her arms were hugging Kira with the fierce maternal affection of a grizzly, but her eyes met Zack's over Kira's head. "You came."

He smiled faintly. "You knew I would."

"Yes. I knew." She gave Kira one final embrace and slowly released her. "It is done?"

"No."

Marna's expression sharpened. "Why not?"

"Because I am not a *chitka*," he said softly.

Her face clouded with anger. "I wanted it d—"
She broke off and then gave a deep, booming
laugh. "No, you are not a *chitka*," she said, shaking
her head. "You never were, Zack. Though in
this case I wish you had been. It would have been
easier for me."

"And for me too. But the easy way is not always
the best way."

Kira was looking from one to the other with exasperation. "I'm still in the room, you know," she
said pointedly. "I have the distinct feeling that I've
just become invisible."

"Go sit down, Kira," Marna said, not looking at
her. "I must talk to Zack for a minute. We have
things to discuss."

Kira turned obediently away and then suddenly
whirled back to face them. "The hell I will. I'm not
an infant to be sent out to play while adults talk."

Marna's eyes widened in surprise and then darkened with a touch of sadness. "It has already begun
then."

"Oh, Marna, I'm sorry," Kira said, instantly contrite. "I didn't mean to snap. It's just that I don't
understand any of this, and both you and Zack are
treating me like a child."

"All right, stay," Marna said with a shrug. "It will
make no difference." She faced Zack, her jaw set a
trifle belligerently. "You accept the *mondava*?"

"I accept it," Zack said quietly. "With all my
heart."

The belligerence suddenly faded, replaced by
weariness. "That goes without saying. It has to be
with all your heart or there is no *mondava*." She

turned away. "It must be done as quickly as possible. I'm finding this very difficult."

"Tonight," Zack said.

Her face took on a sudden fierceness. "No! You've had your chance. You can wait now until we can do it properly and with all due ceremony."

Zack frowned. "The hell I will. We don't even know when that will be and I'm already going crazy."

There was the slightest hint of malicious pleasure in Marna's smile. "How unfortunate. Then you'll just have to arrange matters so the ceremony can take place quite soon, won't you?"

Zack muttered a low oath under his breath. "Has it slipped your memory that right now we have to concentrate on your escape from Tamrovia?"

"I thought you'd both forgotten," Kira said caustically. "You won't mind if I interrupt this cryptic conversation to remind you that we came here to inform Marna we're planning on getting her out of here tomorrow?"

Marna's gaze moved to Zack's face. "How?"

"Tomorrow night there will be a reception at the palace and people will be coming and going constantly. Your guards will be bribed to allow you to be smuggled out of here and through Belajo to the woods south of the city. A helicopter will be waiting there. Kira and I will join you as soon as we can get away from the reception. Then we'll take off. By dawn we should have crossed the border into Switzerland." He turned to Kira. "Are the grounds to the rear of the palace as well guarded as the main gate?"

"Yes," she said thoughtfully. "But you won't have

to take her out either the back or the front." Her eyes met Marna's and she smiled. "There's another way."

Zack's brows lifted. "A flying carpet."

She grinned. "Better. A secret passage in my apartment that leads underneath the grounds and the main gate and into a cave in the woods. All you have to do is arrange to have a car standing by out of sight of the palace."

"A secret passage," Zack repeated, a little smile tugging at his lips. "I should have known. What else could I expect in a situation like this? Gypsies, palaces, and Balkan intrigue. It fits right in. I wonder why I even bothered to formulate an efficient plan."

"It *is* efficient," Marna said slowly. "Just what I would have expected of you, Zack. I will make only one alteration."

Zack frowned. "Alteration?"

"The helicopter pilot will put us down in a clearing that I will designate, about eighty miles from here. He will be ordered to return in twenty-four hours." She smiled calmly. "And *then* he will fly us to Switzerland."

"No!" Zack said. "It's too risky. The entire countryside may be crawling with—"

Marna held up her hand to stop him. "It is the only way I will go."

"Marna, please," Kira pleaded. "I don't know what this is all about, but if Zack thinks it's too dangerous, then I believe you should do as he asks."

A curious smile tugged at Marna's lips. "You trust him?"

Kira met her eyes steadily. "I trust him."

"Good," Marna said. "I trust him, too, but we'll still follow my plan and not his." She patted Kira's cheek gently. "Give in to me in this, little one. It is for the best, I promise you. For this last time, let me be the one to make things as they should be for you."

This last time. The words were weighted with a strange sadness that made Kira vaguely uneasy. "Marna . . ." She stared at her helplessly. Then she turned to Zack, unconsciously squaring her shoulders. "Zack, I think we should do as she wishes. Can't you find some way to make it safe for her? It's only for one night and—"

"All right." The quiet assent surprised her so much that she broke off in mid-sentence. Where she had expected to find resistance, she now found only gentleness and understanding. "Don't look so astounded, love. I know how you feel about Marna." He turned away. "I'll get to work right away rearranging my plans." His gaze met Marna's across the room. "I guess this means you're keeping Kira with you tonight?"

Marna nodded. "Yes. We will have dinner together and talk of the old days and remember. I will send her back to you tomorrow afternoon."

A crooked smile slanted his lips. "I suppose it wouldn't do any good to remind you that Karpathan will consider it a little strange for me to let her leave tonight, when we've put out the story we're a very hot item?"

"Has Karpathan seen you together?"

Zack nodded. "Yes."

Marna smiled faintly. "Then there is no problem.

Karpathan is not a *chitka* either. He has eyes to see what is there and many things not so plain." She paused. "He came to visit me a few times while you were gone."

"He did?" Kira asked, startled. "Why?"

Marna shrugged. "Who knows? He asked no questions. He merely sat and chatted and smiled. He knows I do not trust him. Perhaps he thought to work his magic on me as he does on Stefan."

"Work his magic," Zack repeated thoughtfully. "A curious phrase. Are you crediting him with Rasputin-like powers?"

"I do not know. There are men who are not easy to read," Marna said. "Some men are meant to control the winds and others are meant to be buffeted by them." She looked directly at Zack. "Which do *you* think is Karpathan's destiny?"

"That's a good question," Zack said dryly. "Perhaps I'll invite him to have dinner with me. At least it would be stimulating and I'm evidently to be deprived of what I really want."

"Only temporarily." Marna's sudden smile lit her usually impassive face with warmth. "I thank you for giving me this," she said haltingly. "I can already feel your power. You could have won if you'd cared to do battle."

He shook his head. "Then I truly would have lost. We're not in competition, Marna. I'd be an ungrateful bastard if I didn't realize all I owe you." His eyes lingered for a moment on Kira's bemused face. "Stay with her," he said softly. "Love her, Kira, there's no one who deserves it more."

Kira laughed a little shakily. "I know. I'm just wondering how the devil you do. A few months out of a lifetime fifteen years ago and you're suddenly blood relatives or something."

Zack grinned. "Perhaps you're not far off the mark. The American Indian is supposed to have arrived in North America by crossing the Bering Strait in the dawn of history. Maybe my ancestors and Marna's wandered across Europe and Asia together at one point in time."

Marna looked at him in surprise. "But why are you laughing? That's exactly what happened."

Zack blinked and then shook his head resignedly. "You didn't tell me."

"I do not tell anyone everything," she said. "Life would not be nearly as interesting."

"Just a good deal simpler," Zack murmured. He opened the door. "Enjoy your evening, ladies. I'll see you tomorrow, Kira."

Kira watched the door close behind him with an odd feeling of loneliness.

"Kira."

Marna's voice was soft and so was her expression when Kira turned to face her. "It's only one night, not forever."

Kira smiled mistily. "I don't know what's going on. I don't know what's happening to me."

"You know."

Kira looked into her eyes. "I love him? How could I? I don't even know him."

Marna shrugged. "You know him. He is the other half of you. When the two pieces come together there is no uncertainty. Accept it."

"Marna . . ." Kira suddenly came back into her arms. "I've never felt like this before. Help me."

Marna's hand was gently stroking her hair. "I have helped you. Now you must help me."

Kira's head lifted swiftly. "How?"

"Forget him. Forget him for this one night and be my child again."

Kira gazed at her for a long moment and then slowly nodded. "If that is what you want."

"That is what I want." Marna gave her a quick, affectionate hug and then let her go. She took Kira's hand and drew her over to the couch, pushed her down on the cushioned softness, and sat down beside her. Then she took her hand again with a companionableness that bridged all the years. "Do you know what I first remember about you? You were only a few months old when I came to the palace, and I was frightened, and lonely for my people. You were sleeping when they brought you to me. Then you opened your eyes and I knew I'd never be lonely again. I knew that as long as I had you to love and care for, there would never be loneliness or sadness or any battle I could not win."

Kira felt an aching tightness in her throat. "We didn't win all the battles, Marna, but those we did win were won because you were there with me."

"Talk to me," Marna said softly. "Remember with me."

Kira hesitated, trying to grasp just what it was Marna needed. Then, with absolute certainty, she knew. It was the time for gathering memories and dreams of childhood so they could be stored lovingly away to make room for new dreams, new visions. Marna wanted to be named guardian of those memories because she was afraid she'd have no place in the new dream.

It wasn't true, but Kira knew that words would never convince Marna. She would have to be shown. In the meantime, she would give Marna what she asked. She settled herself more comfortably on the couch, her fingers tightening on the hand of her old friend. "I think one of my very best memories is of the first time you took me to meet your people. I couldn't have been more than three or four, and I was so excited. It was spring and the entire Gypsy camp was bathed in sunlight. The horses' coats were gleaming and the paint on the caravans was so bright it hurt my eyes to look at them. Everyone was laughing and glad to see you. I felt a little shy among all those strangers, but you were holding my hand and I was so proud to be with you. I knew there was nothing to be frightened of as long as . . ."

For many hours they wove tapestries of memories and love and togetherness. The light in the room mellowed and then faded to an intimate dusk as they spoke and remembered and prepared the way for the new harvest to come.

Five

Stefan towered head and shoulders above the small coterie surrounding him. His broad-shouldered form looked very impressive in the medal-bedecked blue uniform and his silver-threaded auburn hair shone as he stood under the magnificent crystal chandelier in the center of the ballroom. He was laughing, his face handsome.

"Brother Stefan appears to be in a good mood tonight," Zack murmured in Kira's ear as they walked across the room in the direction of the elite cluster.

"Well, I'm not," Kira whispered as she smiled brilliantly and nodded to the right and left at acquaintances in the crowd. "I'm so nervous I can scarcely breathe."

"You don't look nervous," Zack said quietly. His gaze ran over her small figure in the delicate pink silk gown. "You look very lovely, the perfect princess."

"Training." She made a face. "I feel like a little girl who wants to go hide under the covers. I'm so scared Marna will be hurt."

"She won't be hurt." Zack's lips thinned to grimness. "I've made it quite clear to my men what will happen if she develops so much as a hangnail from this escape. I guarantee they won't run any risks getting her out of the palace. Just hold on and it will all be over soon. In another hour she should be leaving the palace grounds."

"You're sure the guards won't panic and decide the bribe isn't worth risking Karpathan's anger? It seems impossible that you were able to set up the bribe so quickly."

"They won't panic." His hand reached out to clasp her arm bracingly. "And my men won't panic either. You're the only one who's in a tizzy."

"Well, I'm not accustomed to— Where's Karpathan? I don't see him."

"I do. There he is." Zack nodded toward a corner of the room. "Take it easy. I guarantee he's not at Marna's suite lying in wait with a drawn pistol."

"I wouldn't put it past him. How long do we have to stay?"

"Another two hours should do it."

Stefan glanced up and saw them approaching. He immediately stepped forward and out of the crowd. "Mr. Damon. We have been waiting for you," he said with a jovial smile. "There are any number of people who want to meet you." He glanced reproachfully at Kira. "You shouldn't be so selfish, darling. We haven't seen anything of our guest since you arrived."

Kira forced a smile through clenched teeth. "I'm sorry, Stefan. I didn't realize Zack's arrival would cause such a storm. I've been showing him some of my favorite haunts." She paused before adding deliberately, "And introducing him to my favorite people."

The genial smile faded a little. "Yes, I heard about that." The smile regained its brilliance. "We all admire your loyalty, even if it is a trifle misplaced. I'm sure Mr. Damon realizes that sometimes we're forced to undertake unpleasant tasks for the general good."

Kira kept the smile fixed firmly on her face as she counted to ten under her breath. She should know by now that it did no good to blow up at Stefan. He actually believed every word he uttered. If *he* thought something was for Stefan's good and the good of Tamrovia, then it must be so. He was the king, wasn't he? "I'll try to remember that the next time I visit Marna and watch her pace the floor. She's a *Gypsy*, Stefan. Don't you realize what that means? Freedom is as necessary to her as air to breathe."

"Sandor says she's adjusted very well," Stefan said soothingly. "Don't be so melodramatic, Kira. Mr. Damon will think all Tamrovians are as uncivilized and untamed as you and your friend Marna."

"Marna isn't uncivilized," Kira began hotly. "Her people have a different philosophy, but that doesn't mean—"

Zack's words swiftly cut across hers as his hand tightened warningly on her elbow. "I happen to admire Kira's untamed qualities, Your Majesty. If she derived them from her former nursemaid, then I owe her a vote of thanks." He smiled blandly. "You may have heard rumors that my own background isn't precisely civilized."

For an instant Stefan looked a little uncomfortable. "Well, I'm sure you're—" He broke off, his expression brightening with relief as he spotted his adviser. "Sandor, I was wondering where you were. We must introduce Mr. Damon to our guests."

Karpathan smiled lazily as he inclined his head in acknowledgment. "That was my intention, Stefan. I came as soon as I realized our guest of honor had arrived." He turned to Kira with a graceful bow that still managed to contain a hint of mockery. "You look enchanting this evening, Your Highness."

"Thank you," Kira said. Enchanting. The word sent an unpleasantly reminiscent chord through her as she remembered Marna's remark about Karpathan working his magic on Stefan. Tonight he looked more than capable of doing that. The white tie and tails accented both his height and elegant slenderness and the only note of color in his outfit was the brilliant blue-and-white sash he wore diagonally across his breast. The very simplicity of his clothes only served to emphasize the aura of strength that surrounded him. "I find you enchanting, too, Sandor."

Karpathan's brows lifted in surprise and his lips curved in a slightly whimsical smile. "Thank you . . . I think." He turned to Zack. "I was just speaking to a man I believe you will be fascinated to meet. He's something of a tycoon himself. We do have them in Tamrovia, you know. Perhaps we could leave Kira for Stefan to entertain for a few minutes. I'm sure you wouldn't hear a word the poor man said with her at your side distracting you."

Zack frowned. "I don't know . . ."

"Go on," Kira said quickly. She hadn't been exactly an asset to their enterprise this evening. Zack was probably afraid to leave her alone. It was time she started conducting herself with a little more control. "I'll be fine. I won't even miss you."

He smiled at her with an intimacy that was entirely unfeigned. "You'd better miss me. Or I'll show you just how wild and untamed I can be when I come back." His hand fell from her arm and he turned away. "I won't be long."

She smiled as she watched him cross the room with Karpathan. He moved with a power and confidence that reassured and soothed her even when he wasn't beside her. Nothing could go wrong as long as Zack was here.

"He's a very interesting man," Stefan said thoughtfully. "He appears quite taken with you."

"It's mutual." Kira met his gaze directly. "I assumed you were aware of that. You did assign him an adjoining room."

"Sandor suggested it would be tactful, since you evidently shared similar quarters at his house in Tucson," Stefan said easily. "We wanted the arrangement to be as discreet and pleasant as possible for you."

"Thank you, Stefan." There was a thread of irony in her tone. "I realize that one of your prime missions in life is to save me from the consequences of my own foolishness."

"He's a very important man. If handled correctly, Damon could be a valuable asset to us. I'm very glad you brought him with you." He glanced at her with sudden sharpness. "You realize, of course, that marriage is out of the question. Damon's family background is totally unacceptable."

Kira felt a quick surge of rage. She took a deep, steadying breath. "I expected you to feel that way. In other words, Zack is good enough for me to have an affair with in order to add rubles to the royal coffers, but not good enough to be the father of any Rubinoff progeny."

Stefan's expression was pained. "You don't have to be unpleasantly crude, Kira. You know your position requires certain duties of you."

"I don't know anything—" She broke off in midsentence. She wouldn't let him anger her. It was too dangerous tonight. "I'm thirsty. I think I'll go see if I can find a glass of champagne." She turned away. "I'll see you later, Stefan."

"Kira."

She turned back to see a distinctly uneasy expression on Stefan's face. "You spent last night in Marna's suite."

She stiffened warily. "So?"

"I'm sure Damon resented sharing your attention with anyone so early in your relationship. It's obvious the man is quite possessive of you. You were lucky he didn't take offense and leave Tamrovia in a huff."

She gazed at him in disbelief. "Now you're telling me how to conduct my own love affair?"

"Well, we all know how unthinking and undisciplined you can be. Sandor and I discussed it early this afternoon and we decided it would be best to move Marna to the prison at Belajo tomorrow until Damon leaves Tamrovia. We'll make sure she has special treatment and every comfort. Then you'll be able to give Damon your full attention during his stay."

"Sandor," she repeated dully. She wouldn't have put this plan past Stefan, but he usually moved more slowly and methodically. It must have been Karpathan who had nudged him into such swift action. And she doubted if it was her presence in Damon's bed that was the real issue with her dear cousin. She felt a ripple of chilling panic. Did he suspect something?

"Sandor is very perceptive in these matters," Stefan said. "You'd be wise to be guided by him."

Good heavens, was he offering Karpathan's services as her pimp, she thought hysterically? She had to get control of herself. "I'll consider that advice. You appear to find him very valuable in that capacity." She turned away again. "Perhaps we'll discuss it later."

She was scarcely aware of the next two hours as she drifted from group to group with a bright, meaningless smile pasted on her face. She certainly wasn't conscious of what she said to anyone. Her conversation must not have been too outrageous for no one seemed to be startled or upset with her. She caught glimpses of Zack from time to time, with Karpathan always at his elbow. She had to restrain herself from running to him and nestling close to shut away the icy fear Stefan had instilled in her. No, she had to do her part. She couldn't depend on Zack for everything. But why didn't he break away and come to her? Surely enough time had passed now for them to leave without comment.

She put her fluted champagne glass down carefully on the chest beside the French doors. She couldn't take this any longer. She felt as if her smile were frozen on her face and her stomach full of butterflies. She'd slip out on the terrace a moment and get a breath of air. Perhaps when she came back inside, Zack would be ready to leave.

The air was clear and cold and the stars brilliant in the night sky. She closed the doors behind her and wandered out on the terrace to stand at the stone balustrade and look out over the garden. It was much better out here. There was a peacefulness that was a balm to her raw nerves. She heard the door open behind her and she tensed.

"Are you all right?"

Zack's voice. She relaxed and turned to face him. "I just had to get away for a while. Can we leave now?"

"In a minute." He left the French door open wide as he crossed the terrace toward her. "What's wrong? You looked taut as a bow string. I was worried about you."

"Were you?" She hadn't realized he'd been watching her. The knowledge sent a little current of warmth through her that partially dispelled the chill. She looked up at him. "I was frightened. Stefan told me that Sandor had spoken to him about moving Marna from the palace tomorrow.

Do you suppose he suspects something and has set extra guards on her tonight?"

He shook his head. His hands reached out and cupped her face in his hands. "It's too late even if he has," he said softly. "I received word thirty minutes ago that Marna is safely out of the palace and on her way to the helicopter."

Kira was so relieved that she went limp. "Oh, thank God!" she said on a long drawn-out breath. "How did you—?"

"Another bribe. I arranged to have one of the guards get a message to me. I knew you'd be worried until you knew for sure."

"Thank you." She could feel the foolish tears well up in her eyes. It was such a wonderfully thoughtful thing for him to have done. "I feel better now. When can we join her?"

"Soon. First we have to provide a logical reason for withdrawing from Stefan's charming festivities."

"What reason?"

He smiled faintly. "Lust. It's the most convincing reason I can think of—besides being the most enjoyable." He slowly lowered his head toward her mouth. "I left the door open. I don't think anyone will be rude enough to interrupt us, but it should be fairly clear to any passerby what we're doing here, even though they can't see us too well because of the shadows." His lips feathered hers, sipping with a teasing delicacy that caused her to arch up to him with helpless abandon. "I missed you last night. I've never had you in my bed, but still I missed you."

"Did you?" She would never have guessed it.

When she had returned to the suite after lunch his manner had been casual to the point of being brotherly.

His tongue brushed her lower lip. "I kept remembering the scent of you and how your breasts tasted. I lay there all night aching and thinking what I'd do to you when we were together. When you walked into the suite I was within an inch of throwing you down and . . ." He drew a deep breath. "But I knew I wouldn't be able to stop until the ache was gone, and I wasn't sure if that would be in hours . . ." His lips hardened as he kissed her with almost bruising passion. "Or days . . . or weeks." His left hand moved from her cheek, down her throat, and under the silk of her bodice. "And we had a prior engagement tonight." His warm palm closed over her naked breast and she inhaled sharply. "I love to feel you swell under my hand," he said softly, his gaze dark and intent on her face. "I can feel your nipple harden and tauten, pushing against my skin. Do you know how it makes me feel to know I can do that to you? I can't wait until I have you back at the lodge. I want to know that anytime I wish, I can just reach out and slip my hand beneath all these silky trappings and you'll be as ready for me as I am for you." His palm rubbed slowly back and forth. She gasped. "I want to make you want me so much that you're as crazy for it as I am."

Her hands dug into his shoulders. "Zack, please, not . . ."

He drew a deep, shuddering breath, but his hand continued to move on her breast as if unable to stop. "I know, but I don't want to—" He broke off. "All right." His hand reluctantly slipped out of the bodice of the gown. "I'm sorry. I realize it's not the time or the place." He turned away. "But it sure as hell better be soon, dammit. I can't take much more of this."

"Neither can I," Kira said shakily. Her breasts were still swollen and taut and she wanted his hand back on her to ease that aching.

"You go on ahead. I'll join you in the suite as soon as I'm in a little better shape to face Stefan's guests."

Her cheeks were hot as she turned away. She was sure her arousal was almost as obvious as Zack's. "Perhaps using lust as an excuse wasn't such a good idea," she said with a quavering little laugh. "I'll see you in a few minutes then."

"Kira."

She turned to look at him over her shoulder.

"It wasn't lust."

"I know," she said softly as she moved toward the French doors. "I know that, Zack."

Kira had already changed from her formal wear to jeans, a thigh-length beige sweater, and soft suede boots when Zack opened the door to the suite. He had also changed and was wearing charcoal-gray cords and a black sweatshirt, and carrying his suede jacket. "Ready?"

She nodded as she slipped on a black leather flight jacket and stuffed her passport and wallet into the pocket. She cast a wistful glance at the photographs on the walls. It hadn't been difficult leaving them before, because she had always known she would be back. But after tonight she couldn't be sure she would ever be permitted to return.

"I'll try to arrange to have them smuggled out and brought to you later." Zack's understanding gaze was on her face.

She smiled with an effort. "They aren't really valuable except to me." She turned away. "Stefan will probably be so angry he'll make a bonfire of them anyway. Karpathan will no doubt be delighted to supply the match."

"We could try to take them with us."

"Too bulky. I don't have the negatives. Stefan destroyed them when he took away my camera. It may come down to having to move fast and free." She shrugged. "It's all right. I knew when I started this that there were things I'd have to give up. Freeing Marna is worth it."

"Even if it means giving up your country?"

"I never actually had a country to give up." She smiled sadly. "Stefan and my parents locked me up in a nice, insulated glass bubble and never let me out of it. Every time I thought I had found the key, they changed the lock." Her gaze went to the picture of the union leader, Naldona. "When he spoke at that meeting he was talking about all the things I wanted for Tamrovia. How I wished I could help the way he did," she whispered. "God, I wanted that."

She didn't realize Zack was behind her until his hands closed gently on her upper arms. "We have to go."

"I know." She stepped away from him and straightened her shoulders. "I probably wouldn't have made a very good activist anyway. I managed to mess things up beautifully for Naldona the only time I tried to do something constructive for Tamrovia." She crossed the room to the paneled wall of bookshelves. "The entrance to the secret passage is right here. This candelabra beside the fifth shelf." She turned the sconce to the left and the entire bookcase swiveled slowly away from the wall, revealing a dark opening only a few feet wide. "There it is."

"It's practically noiseless," Zack said as he peered warily into the darkness. "You must keep the mechanism very well oiled."

She grinned as she turned on the flashlight to reveal a curving flight of narrow stone steps. "Oh yes, sort of a sacred duty passed on to me by Lance."

"Sacred duty?"

"Well, perhaps *sacred* isn't precisely the right word. This apartment used to belong to my brother Lance." She entered the passage and waited until Zack joined her before turning a sconce on the wall that was identical to the one in the suite. This time she turned it to the right. The bookcase swung slowly shut, imprisoning them in the narrow confines of the passageway. "You've probably heard that Lance was slightly wild before he married."

"Slightly?" Zack asked dryly. "I believe the tabloids referred to him as Lusty Lance."

She nodded as she began to lead the way carefully down the staircase. "Well, Lance discovered this passageway when he was a teenager and used it to slip in and out of the palace when he wanted to keep a rendezvous with one of his ladies. He told me about it when I visited him in Sedikhan. When I came back I pestered Stefan to let me change suites. It made things much easier for Marna and me, when we couldn't stand it here any longer and needed to get away from all this stifling protocol."

"Is this the only secret passage in the palace?"

"As far as Marna and I could discover, and this one was apparently unused and forgotten for decades until Lance found it." She had reached the bottom of the staircase and turned to him with a finger to her lips. "We'll have to be quiet now. This passage runs alongside the ballroom, down some stairs to the dungeon, and under the grounds to the woods across from the main gate. I don't know how thick the walls are in this part of the passage, but we'd better not take a chance."

He nodded and followed her noiselessly as she turned and made her way swiftly through the twisting passageway.

The lights of the Mercedes splayed out over the countryside, picking up the blue-and-silver gleam of the helicopter in the meadow to the right of the dirt road on which they were traveling. A small Porsche was parked beside it and its doors suddenly opened as the Mercedes came to a halt. Two men emerged.

Kira's heart gave a little jerk as Marna was helped from the car by the man who had gotten out of the backseat. She was safe! She didn't realize how tense she'd been until she saw Marna's big frame silhouetted against the headlights.

Zack's gaze was on her face. "I told you she would be safe."

"I know, but it seemed impossible that everything could go so smoothly," she said, blinking back the sudden tears. "It wasn't that I didn't trust you."

His hand tightened around her wrist. "Thank you for saying that. It means a great deal to me." He opened the door. "Let's get this little odyssey under way, shall we? Even if we're destined to spend the next day or so in Tamrovia, I'll feel better once we get out of the city." He helped Kira out of the car and turned to Marna. "Have you changed your mind about letting us go straight through to Switzerland tonight, Marna?"

"No," Marna said serenely. "Switzerland has been there for a long, long time. I trust it will still be there tomorrow."

He shook his head. "I was afraid of this. Get into the helicopter, ladies. I have a few instructions to give my men before we leave."

He joined them a few minutes later, carefully storing a small metal suitcase in the back of the helicopter. The taillights of the cars were disappearing down the road and the meadow was very dark and eerily silent.

"You're going to fly it yourself? I thought you were going to have a pilot put us down and then come back for us."

He shook his head. "I don't like the idea of being stranded with no transportation in case things don't proceed as smoothly as Marna thinks they will."

"Perhaps I should fly it? I know Tamrovia terrain better than you do, and I'm quite a good pilot."

"I'm sure you are, but I need something to do." He sat down in the pilot's seat and passed Marna a navigation map. "I'd appreciate it if you'd try to designate our landing site on the map. It will be easier than hit-or-miss."

"Certainly." Marna opened the map and her index finger went unhesitatingly to a point on the map. "Does that help?"

Zack's lips were twitching as he turned on the ignition. "It helps. Tell me, did you actually read the map or did you divine it?"

"What difference does it make?"

"No difference. I was just curious." The rotors were whirring loudly and he had to raise his voice to be heard. "I'd set it down there regardless."

"Of course you would. Why should you do anything else? We've already determined that you're not a *chitka*."

A low, amused laugh was Zack's only answer as the helicopter ponderously lifted off, turned in a ninety-degree circle, and headed north.

Six

Zack turned off the ignition, reached for the utility lantern/flashlight on the floor beside him, then opened the door of the helicopter. "Your charming sylvan glade seems deserted."

"It won't be for long," Marna said serenely. "They know we're coming."

"I won't ask how." Zack had come around and opened the passenger door. He lifted first Marna and then Kira to the grass. "But I would like to inquire who you think will be comin—"

"Marna!" A giant of a man stepped out of the darkness into the circle of light from the flashlight. "We knew those *chitkas* couldn't hold you." A scowl deepened the lines of the man's rough-hewn features. "But you took your time about breaking free of them. We were wondering when you would come back to us."

"Paulo." There was deep affection in Marna's murmur as she hugged the large man. She turned to Zack. "You remember my brother Paulo."

"I remember," Zack said. He smiled warmly at Paulo as he shook the man's gigantic paw. Paulo Debuk had changed very little over the years. His dark, full beard was peppered with gray now, but his big-boned body was still as lithe and powerful as Zack remembered it from years ago. He was dressed in scuffed boots, an old suede vest, a tattered full-sleeved tan shirt, and rough denim trousers, and he wore this shabby apparel with an air of careless majesty that even Stefan would have envied. "We used to hunt these hills together," Zack said. "Is hunting still such a passion with you, Paulo?"

"Now more than ever," Paulo said, smiling in an odd way. "The hills are full of strange and interesting prey these days. It's quite a challenge to stalk it, but as yet I haven't bothered to bring any home."

Zack's eyes narrowed on Paulo's bearded face. "Sounds intriguing. I wish I had time to join you."

Paulo suddenly laughed. "No, you'll be too busy with the little one to hunt with me on this visit." He turned to Kira and enveloped her in a bear hug, whirling her in a circle. "How are you, Kira? You bagged big game yourself, eh?"

"Has anyone ever told you about women's liberation?" Kira asked tartly. "I never could persuade you to take *me* hunting."

"It was not because you were a female," he protested as he set her on her feet. "To hunt, one must have the proper instincts. If I had taken you with me, all you would have done was snap pretty pictures."

"And Zack has the right instincts, I suppose?"

Paulo looked at Zack over Kira's head. "Yes, he has the instincts. He knows when to kill, when to capture, and when to set free. It's in the blood." He turned back to Marna. "I will take Zack to the *saldana* to spend the night. You and Kira go back to the encampment. We will speak of the *mondava* in the morning."

"We need to camouflage the helicopter before daybreak," Zack said. "And I have a shortwave radio to keep in contact with my people in Belajo. I want to bring that with me to the camp."

Paulo nodded. "I'll send someone to pick it up tomorrow before dawn. I'll put a guard on the helicopter tonight."

"A guard? They probably don't even know Marna's escaped yet."

Paulo shrugged. "It doesn't hurt to be cautious." He ruffled Kira's hair playfully. "Run along with Marna, little one. We'll take care of everything from now on. You don't have to be afraid."

"I'm *not* afraid." Kira's hands clenched into fists at her sides in frustration. "And I may be little, but I'm *not* a child."

Paulo's laughter boomed out. "We are all children. Some only more so than others." He tugged teasingly at a lock of her auburn hair. "Enjoy your childhood, Kira."

"No," Zack said quietly. "We're not being fair." He took a step closer to her and his eyes were deep and soft in the lantern light. "I know all this is confusing and annoying to you. I promise it won't continue to be that way for very much longer. I'll try to explain it all to you tomorrow. Okay?"

She felt the now familiar melting sensation attack her muscles and cause her breathing to quicken. "Okay."

The tip of his index finger touched her cheek in the lightest of caresses. "You're being very patient with us."

"I never even knew I possessed an iota of patience until the last few days. I'm learning new things all the time about my inner resources." She turned to Marna. "Shall we go on to the camp? Evidently I've just been told to run along and play in the sandbox again."

Marna smiled. "It is best. You will see. Come on, the camp is through that grove of poplars."

Kira lifted her hand resignedly in farewell to Zack and Paulo, and muttered "Good night" before falling into step with Marna.

Zack's gaze followed her as she swiftly strode with Marna toward the grove. When her figure was lost to him in the shadowy darkness of the trees, he turned toward Paulo.

"A time to capture and a time to set free," Paulo reminded him softly.

Zack clapped him on the shoulder. "I know, my friend, but in this particular instance my priorities are confused. My hunting instincts are being sublimated by the mating instinct. I'll be damned glad when all this is over."

"It is important to Marna. She has planned this for a long time." Paulo waved his hand. "It's only one more night. I have an excellent brandy at the *saldana*. Maybe we'll get drunk and you'll forget about little Kira for the night."

"It's worth a try," Zack said. He was willing to try anything to avoid another night like the last one he'd spent. He seemed to be in a permanent state of arousal these days, and he had only to look at Kira to have that arousal sharpen to an aching feverishness. "By all means, lead on to the *saldana*."

The crisp fallen leaves crunched under Kira's suede boots and she could see her breath form misty clouds as she walked beside Marna through the grove. The stars looked different here in the woods than they had from the terrace. Had it been only a few hours since she'd stood on the terrace at the palace? she wondered. She felt shocked because that scene seemed to belong to a different century and certainly to a different world.

"What is a *saldana*?" she asked suddenly.

"It is a place apart," Marna said. "When there is a need, one of the caravans is pulled a short distance from the rest of the camp to insure complete privacy."

"A need?"

"Grief or a soul search or a *mondava*." She paused. "You will be with Zack at the *saldana* tomorrow night."

Kira swallowed. "I will? How nice of you to tell me."

Marna's eyes were suddenly probing. "You have promised to belong to him. Is that not so?"

"Yes."

"It is not against your will? You wish to be in his bed?"

"No, it's not against my will, and yes, I wish to be in his bed." Heaven knew that was the truth. She was so acutely aware of him, just the light touch of his finger on her cheek had caused a ripple of desire to invade every secret part of her.

"Then that's all that is important. The understanding will come in time," Marna said. "It is all part of the *mondava*."

"Are you going to tell me what this *mondava* is?" Kira asked dryly. "Evidently I figure in it prominently and I appear to be the only one around here who is ignorant about it."

"You don't know? I thought Zack would tell you." Marna smiled wryly. "No, I thought he would show you."

"He was just as closemouthed as you were," Kira said.

Marna frowned. "You must not go into it without knowledge. I did not mean for that to happen."

"Zack said it meant the 'forever bonding' or 'everlasting bonding' in your dialect."

"Everlasting," Marna said softly. "Yes, that is what it means. It is the coming together. The sealing of two souls who have been parted. There is a proper time for all things, and when the time is right there comes the *mondava*." Her glance met Kira's. "Not only the souls are united but also the bodies. Sometimes the merging does not come at one and the same time, but then one always follows the other. You must not worry if Zack seems to forget the soul for the body. The other will come."

"Will it?" Kira drew a deep, shaky breath.

"Marna, for heaven's sake, how do you know? Zack may only be aware of the physical aspect of the *mondava*. I offered myself to him on a silver platter to get you out of Tamrovia. He may think the *mondava* is something like the gestures of hospitality some primitive people made in offering their women to visiting men. Remember, he only spent a short time with your tribe and may not fully understand the *mondava*."

Marna shook her head. "He understands."

"Marna . . ." It was no use. Kira could tell by the set of Marna's jaw that she had made up her mind and no amount of arguing was going to change it. She was obviously convinced Zack was the only mate for Kira and was proceeding to effect the union in her own unique, inexorable fashion. She wouldn't even consider the possibility that Zack might not be ready to commit himself to anything but a physical relationship.

But Kira's argument *was* valid, dammit, even if Marna wouldn't admit it. Zack had certainly been quick enough to reject the possibility of marriage to her, she remembered with a pang. Their relationship had deepened and grown enormously in the short time they had known each other, but it didn't mean Zack had changed his mind. Evidently this ritual Marna was arranging was equivalent to a tribal marriage ceremony. Legal or not, Zack had an innate respect for tribal rituals and would regard this one as binding. Oh, Lord, she hadn't meant to trap him. And there was no doubt that the desire tormenting them both was the bait for the trap. She couldn't let such a thing happen to Zack. "When is this ceremony?" she asked suddenly.

"Tomorrow at nightfall," Marna said. "We will spend the day preparing you." She paused. "Of course the *mondava* also signals the end of child-hood for a woman and the beginning of maturity."

Ah, Kira thought, now she understood why Marna had been so melancholy last night. She believed Kira would give herself totally to Zack and forsake all those she'd loved before.

"We're going to have to talk about your feelings, Marna," Kira said gently. "Yes, we need to talk about a good many things other than memories."

"The *mondava*," Marna said flatly.

"In a manner of speaking. About maturity, any-way. It will wait, though. You've already given me too much to think about right now."

"It will all come clear. Tomorrow night at the *mondava*."

"Kira."

It was Zack's whisper.

She woke instantly from the light sleep into which she'd fallen only a few hours before. She lifted her head from the pillow and saw Zack's dark silhouette framed against the pearly gray light of predawn coming through the opening at the front of the wagon. Kira cast a glance at the large form on the mattress next to her own. Marna hadn't stirred at Zack's low call.

Kira threw off the blanket and came swiftly to her knees on the pallet. She searched in the shad-ows of the caravan until she found her jacket and suede boots, and then crawled quickly to the front of the wagon.

Zack lifted her from the seat to the ground with careful and soundless strength. "I'm glad I finally found you. I think I peered into every wagon in camp. Put on your boots." He waited while she pulled them on. It wasn't nearly as cold as it had been last night, even though she noticed that the huge campfire, which was the heart of the ring of caravans surrounding it, had burned down to gray ashes and flickering embers.

There was a touch of impatience in Zack's face as he took her hand. "Come on, let's get the hell out of here." His voice was almost rough and it slightly startled her. She had never seen Zack impatient or rough. She gazed at him bemusedly as he pulled her away from the camp and through the woods. Then they were climbing a hill with a speed that made her legs ache a little by the time they reached the summit.

The sun had not yet risen and within the cluster of trees at the crest of the hill his face was still shadowed and unreadable as she faced him. "Zack? What is it? Is something wrong?"

"Dear heaven, yes, something is wrong," he said in a husky tone of voice. His arms enfolded her with a crushing power that took her breath away. If there had been any left to take away. When she'd been brought with passionate violence against Zack's bold arousal, she'd lost both composure and breath in one swoop. "This is what's wrong." His hands moved down to cup her buttocks and bring her closer still. His hips began to move against her in a slow, undulating movement that was mindlessly primitive. "I can't take it anymore. I thought I could last until Marna's damn ceremony tonight, but I can't do it. It's been too long already and I'm *hurting*." His breath was coming in harsh gasps as his hands clenched on her soft, rounded flesh. "I tried everything last night. I counted a million damn sheep. I kept Paulo up half the night telling stories until he dozed off. I even tried to get drunk." His laugh held an edge of desperation. "Indians are supposed to be susceptible to firewater, but it didn't faze me." His eyes closed and his hands splayed out with a tactile yearning, rubbing and smoothing gently. "Maybe I was high already."

She certainly was, she realized. She was dizzy and helpless from the sensations he was engendering with every touch. She could detect the faint scent of musk and soap and brandy that clung to his body. She had been a little chilly before, but she was burning up now. Her breath was coming in little gasps, as if she were being touched rhythmically by an electric charger. "Zack . . ."

His eyes opened and he glared down at her with an intensity that stopped the words in her throat. "*Say* it, dammit."

She gazed up at him in bewilderment. "Say what?"

"Say yes. Say I can have you. Right now, with no more of this god-awful waiting. Say that I can stop hurting."

He *was* hurting. She could see the agony that tautened his features and caused the skin to tighten over his cheekbones. And she could help him. The knowledge sent a flowing warmth through her to temper with pure joy the white-hot passion she was experiencing. She could stop his hurting, take away the hunger born of pain and bring him pleasure, then peace. "Oh, yes, Zack," she said softly. "Please. Now."

His breath was released in a little explosion. "Thank heaven! I know I'm being a bast—" He broke off. "I'll try to make up for it later." He was drawing her closer with trembling arms. "Just come here and let me love you, Kira. Just let me love you."

His hands were at the belt of her jeans; his attempt at unfastening them was oddly clumsy. The zipper made a soft, silky hiss as it slid down. His hands slipped beneath denim and silk to touch her, sending ripples of shock through her system. His palms were cold, but her own body heat quickly transferred warmth to them.

His nails raked lightly over the curve of her buttocks before moving around to caress the smoothness of her belly with hands shaking with eagerness. "Soft. Lord, you're so soft and sweet. I want to—" His hand moved down to the apex of her thighs and he touched her with a gentleness at odds with the roughness that had preceded it. "I haven't seen you here," he said hoarsely. "When I was lying on that mattress last night, I could imagine every other part of you, because I'd seen how beautiful you were at the lodge." His fingers found the place they were seeking.

She gave a low cry as he pressed and then began to rotate the spot slowly. Her eyes were staring blindly up at him and she had to clutch his shoulders or she would have fallen.

"Not here. I couldn't imagine how you looked or

what response you'd give me when I did this."
There was savage joy glittering in his eyes. "But
now I'm going to see you and touch you . . ." He
pressed again and she jerked forward, arching
helplessly toward him. "And pleasure you until you
go out of your mind."

She was already out of her mind. She felt as if
every single nerve ending were on fire. She was
tingling in the strangest places. The centers of her
palms were throbbing and her toes wanted to curl.
He stepped back from her, took off his jacket, and
spread it on a pile of beech leaves on the ground.
Then he was pulling her down on her knees on the
coat to face him. The dry leaves rustled beneath his
coat as he shifted to remove her jacket too. "Damn,
I'll probably give you pneumonia. Are you cold?"

"If there's one thing I'm not, it's cold," she murmured. Her hands were quivering as she pulled her
sweater over her head and threw it aside. "I'm
burning up!"

"I'll try to keep you burning up." He stopped her
as she started to unfasten the front opening of her
bra. "Let me. I've been looking forward to undress-
ing you. It will be like seeing a flower unfold, petal
by petal." He laughed huskily. "If I can make my
damn hands stop trembling."

They were still trembling as he opened the catch
and slid the straps over her shoulders, as he slowly
slipped the lacy scrap of material down her arms.
Then he drew a shuddering breath, his gaze
caressing the full swollen mounds. His eyes
remained fixed compulsively on her as he pulled
his sweatshirt off and threw it on top of her
sweater. "Come here."

His chest, bronzed, heavily muscled, feathered with a wedge of dark hair, looked deliciously soft and springy to her. She slowly leaned forward and his hands grasped her shoulders. Her head fell back and her eyes closed as he rubbed his chest back and forth against her with a sinuous catlike movement. "Zack . . ." She didn't even realize she had murmured his name. The hair on his chest was a soft, sensuous abrasion against her nipples as he moved. She could feel the muscles of her abdomen twist and knot, and the trembling of her body grew violent.

"You're sure you're not cold?" Zack muttered as his warm tongue moved against her ear.

"I'm not *cold*." He couldn't seem to comprehend such a simple fact. "I'm about to go up in smoke. Why do you—" She broke off as his lips crushed hers with a force and passion that seared through her like a burning brand.

He lay her back on the coat, his hands drawing off her jeans and panties in one clean motion. His head lifted and he looked down at her. He sat back on his heels. His eyes were dark and almost glazed with need as they bored into her. "You look like a cossack and an empress all at once lying there entirely nude except for those boots."

She hadn't been aware that she still had them on. She watched bemusedly as he pulled the right suede boot off and tossed it aside. His hand cupped one bare foot and rubbed the arch, massaging it gently. "You have strong, supple feet. I like that. Your entire body is strong and firm and womanly." She was experiencing little shooting sensations from her arch to her calf. She had never heard that the foot could be an erogenous zone, she realized hazily. She shouldn't have been surprised. She probably didn't have a spot on her body that wasn't an erogenous zone if Zack touched it. His big hands were sliding up her calves now, his fingers massaging and exploring at the same time.

Then he was moving between her legs, parting her thighs gently while gazing at her most intimate part with eyes so dark and intent that she felt as if he were touching her there. "That's what I wanted to see. You're as beautiful here as everywhere else. Now when I'm thinking about you, I'll know and be able to visualize—" He broke off. "But I won't have to visualize anything anymore." His hand reached up and cupped her with a loving possession that made her throat tighten with emotion. "All I'll have to do is turn over and pull the sheet down and look at you." His fingers caressed her slowly, his narrowed eyes intent on the response he caused with every movement. His gaze lifted to meet hers as he slowly lowered his head. "I'll be able to rub my cheek against you and feel how warm and . . ."

His words were muffled, but she wouldn't have been able to hear them anyway. Her head was thrashing back and forth in an agony of hunger. His tongue . . . Her back arched and she cried out brokenly.

Then he was moving over her, his eyes wild and hot and his chest laboring harshly. "Kira. I *need* you. I don't think I can wait any longer." His hands were working at the belt of his pants. "Is it all right?"

All right? she echoed to herself. She was aching

with a hunger that seemed to have gone on forever. "Hurry," she said. "For heaven's sake, *hurry.*"

He was gone. Stripping quickly, tossing his clothes haphazardly onto the ground. She had a vague impression of powerful thighs, tight buttocks—exquisite masculinity—but had no time to assimilate anything else before he was with her again, parting her thighs and sliding between them. Stroking and petting her lovingly, he looked down at her with desire and heat and a vulnerability that startled her. She had always been the vulnerable one since she had met Zack. Yet now she knew he was open and pleading and totally in her hands. With this knowledge came a sense of protectiveness that was fierce in its intensity. Her hands fell to his hips and she felt the ripple and surge of his muscles beneath her palms. "Zack . . . Love me."

He slowly bent forward, his eyes never leaving hers. He nudged against her gently and she could see the wild drumming of the pulse in his temple. His lips moved in a gossamer-soft caress across her mouth. Sweetness, gentleness, a honeycomb of joy. "Open. Let me come in, love. We have to be together."

She opened her mouth and his tongue plunged into it with a wild hardness that surprised her after his gentle overture. He groaned into her throat and she felt his entire body tense with unbearable strain. "Together." He had lifted his lips a fraction from hers and each syllable of the word had been another kiss. His hips plunged forward as his tongue entered her mouth once again.

Pain. Sharp. Startling. Then it was gone, but the

hunger was still there. Zack was moving slowly, carefully. What a beautiful fullness. Hot and heavy. Yet after the first moment it wasn't enough. There was something else waiting for her. Her palms moved restlessly on his hips. She loved the feel of his skin beneath her hands. She wanted to run them all over him and feel the textures. But not now. Now she had to find that something . . . She lunged upward and Zack gave a low cry, as if he had been stung by a whip.

"Kira, I don't want to hurt you . . ." She lunged again and his back arched in an agony of pleasure. He closed his eyes. "All right, but you must tell me if you want me to stop." His husky laugh held a touch of desperation. "I only hope I can still hear you."

He plunged forward with a power and passion that robbed her of breath and then unleashed a fiery rhythm that turned her mindless with sensation. How could anything be this tempest-driven? His hands were beneath her buttocks, lifting her to greater closeness, and his eyes opened to stare down at her blindly.

Together. The word was radiant with beauty. She hadn't realized it until this moment. Closeness and striving for greater unity. The rhythm breaking through barriers to emotion she never had known existed. For it was emotion and not just sensation, she realized dimly. They had passed the point of hunger and were reaching for something beyond. *Mondava?* Part of it, perhaps. She couldn't analyze anything when she was so close . . . Then she was *there* in a burst of radiance that illuminated the world. She heard his low, hoarse cry above her. *Zack. Mondava. Together.*

He was holding her with trembling arms, resting against her, his chest rising and falling heavily. He kissed her tenderly, a silent joining filled with peace, gratitude, sweetness. "I'm too heavy. I must be crushing you." He moved off her with a smile that lit his face with gentleness. "Thank you."

He sat up and a little away from her. He was framed against a dawn shot with pink and gold and magenta, and she wanted to keep looking at him forever. He was all sleek bronze power and rippling muscle and seemed to be an integral part of the sky and the forest of maple and beech trees wreathed in the scarlet and gold of autumn.

"You're not saying anything. Are you all right?"

"I'm wonderful." She sat up with a grin. "And so are you."

He frowned. "I hope your first time wasn't a disappointment. I wasn't that great, you know. I'll do better now that—" He broke off. "Do you know how beautiful you are sitting there? The sunlight is turning your hair the same shade as those maple leaves." She reached for her sweater and he frowned again. "Don't you like me looking at you?"

She smiled. She had never imagined Zack could be even the slightest bit insecure. "I feel perfectly natural and at ease with you." It was true. It was as though she had sat before him naked and joyously uninhibited a thousand times like this.

"Then why are you—"

She held up her hand to stop him. "For the very pedestrian reason that *now* I'm cold."

"Damn! Of course you are." He was suddenly

kneeling beside her. He picked up her bra and slipped it on her. He quickly fastened it with hands that were much steadier than when he had taken it off.

Her sweater followed and he was reaching for her jeans when she stopped him. "I'll do the rest."

"No," he said curtly. "We have to get you dressed as soon as possible. As it is, I've probably made you ill. Why the hell didn't you stop me?"

She stared at him bemusedly as he pulled up her jeans and fastened them swiftly. "I didn't think of it. I don't believe I was thinking at all at that particular moment."

"Well, I should have thought of it." He jammed her left foot into her boot and then smoothed the soft suede over her ankle. "If I had been thinking at all." Then he was putting her right foot into the other boot. "All I was doing was feeling, dammit. I didn't care about anything but stopping that hellish . . ." His voice trailed off as he looked up at her. "I'm sorry, Kira. Will you forgive me?"

"There's nothing to forgive," she said softly. "I don't even know why you think there should be. You're right, I could have said no at any moment and I think you would have stopped." She paused. "I didn't say no."

"I didn't give you much opportunity, did I? I practically kidnapped you from the caravan, pulled you up the hill, and demanded—"

Her fingers swiftly covered his lips. "I'm *not* a victim. You insult me by insinuating that I'd let myself become one. You took nothing I didn't want to give." She smiled. "Now, don't you think *you'd* better get dressed? You're the one who's going to catch cold."

"I seldom feel the cold," he said, still gazing at her intently. "You have every right to be angry with me, you know. I should have waited for the ceremony tonight. I cheated you."

"You didn't cheat me. The ceremony was Marna's idea, not mine. I think I like this better anyway. What happened here was just between the two of us. No mysterious traditions, no *mondava*."

"You're wrong. The *mondava* was here. We merely anticipated it."

He was speaking of the physical joining, she realized with a pang. Now that he'd had her, he might not want to go through Marna's binding, formal ritual. "I've been meaning to speak to you. Marna and I had a talk last night." She looked fixedly at the trunk of a beech tree beyond his shoulder. "She explained about the *mondava* ceremony. Perhaps it would be a good idea if we didn't go through with it."

"The hell you say." Zack's voice was so violent that her gaze ricocheted back to his face. His expression was as hard and grim as his tone. "I think you'd better reconsider. We made a deal, dammit. I know I've just acted with all the tact and skill of a caveman, but that doesn't mean I'll always be that crude. You don't have to marry me, but it won't stain the family escutcheon to go through with this ceremony. It's not even legal in any other country or society. You can at least give me the *mondava*." He stood up and quickly began to pull on his clothes. "The ceremony will go through on schedule. Get used to the idea."

She was gazing bewilderedly at him. "Zack, you don't understand. It was you—"

He made a movement with the edge of his hand like the slicing of a knife. It was a curiously Indian gesture, the first she had seen him make. "It's decided. The discussion is over." He turned and strode swiftly away, leaving her to stare after him with a dazed look on her face.

She'd had no idea her words would touch off such an explosion. It appeared that Zack was aware that the ceremony tonight constituted a commitment and wasn't at all averse to it. She felt a sudden surge of happiness so intense she was a little dizzy. He must have some feeling for her, other than desire, if that volatile break in Zack's usually tranquil demeanor was anything to go by.

She jumped to her feet and gathered up both Zack's jacket and her own. She stood a moment and looked out over the hills, breathing in the aromatic scent of pines and earth and the myriad subtle fragrances that composed this autumn world. There was just the faintest tinge of scarlet left in the heavens. Soon it, too, would be replaced by the deep cerulean blue of the morning. She had a fleeting memory of Zack silhouetted against that sky and felt again a great, buoyant joy. Together.

She turned and walked swiftly down the hill toward the Gypsy encampment. She had always loved to visit Marna's people, from the time she was a tiny child. It was like taking a step back in time, with its brightly painted wagons and well-groomed horses. The tribe had adamantly refused to embrace the conveniences of motor vehicles and continued to travel the countryside as their ancestors had done for centuries. It was very soothing to leave the tensions of the modern world for a place where tradition and simple affection were more important than position and wealth.

People were awakening, preparing for the new day when Kira walked into the camp. Marna was standing by the wagon talking to Paulo and broke off in mid-sentence as Kira came toward her. Paulo gave Kira a puckish grin and a casual wave before he turned and strolled away.

Marna's eyes searched Kira's face and then dropped to Zack's coat draped across her arm. "It is done then," she said quietly.

Kira nodded and unconsciously braced herself for an explosive reaction.

"It was with your will?"

Kira nodded again and met her Marna's gaze steadily. "Yes, I couldn't have been more willing. I'm sorry you're disappointed, but . . ."

Marna's impatient gesture cut her short. "*I* do not matter. The *mondava* exists. That is all that is important." She smiled in a slightly rueful way. "Besides, perhaps it was not the ceremony itself but my wish to exert my will over Zack's that made me so determined. I should have known he would not submit meekly to my controlling the situation. *Disek*s make their own rules and customs." Her smile widened and there was the faintest glint of respect in her eyes. "But I didn't expect him to creep into the wagon at night and steal you away from beside me. That took a Gypsy boldness. I think we trained him too well when he was with us."

"He didn't steal me. He called," Kira said gently. "I believe that for the rest of my life I'll come whenever he calls me."

"It's so strong already? Ah, well, it is only what I expected. Come, we'll have breakfast and then we will begin to prepare you for tonight. Perhaps it's best Zack decided not to tolerate my interference. Now you will be able to concentrate on the soul tonight, instead of the body."

Would she, indeed? Kira somehow doubted it. Her body was still exquisitely sensitive and became even more so when she remembered Zack's hands moving . . . She drew a deep, shaky breath. "I really wouldn't count on my being preoccupied with the soul tonight, Marna."

Marna's dark eyes were suddenly twinkling. "Maybe I should have said you'd be able to concentrate on the soul as well as the body. As for me, today I'm going to enjoy myself. I will talk to the women, and laugh, and be a Gypsy again."

Marna looked years younger and as free and irresponsible as Paulo. She had exchanged the neat black dress she always wore outside the encampment for bright clothing. The full blue skirt and yellow cotton blouse she wore now made her appear almost another person. Kira had never really thought about Marna's age. She had always been merely Marna, as ageless and steady as these hills around them. Now Kira suddenly realized that Marna was only in her early forties.

"You really miss this life, don't you, Marna? You

gave up so much when you left your people to take care of me."

"I gained so much," Marna corrected. "But it is good that they are still here for me now."

But they wouldn't be here for her for very long. She would have to leave her people and her country and go into exile again. There was no question that it was entirely Kira's fault. Marna had been drawn into her problems through duty and devotion and now was going to have to suffer for it. "Oh, Marna, I wish—"

Marna's big hand caressed her cheek in a gesture that was half-pat, half gentle slap. "How many times have I told you that it is useless to wish for things. You either do something to get what you want or accept what you have. Stop worrying about me. I will enjoy what I have while I have it. It is the Gypsy way. My way."

Kira's expression betrayed how troubled she felt. "That's not good enough. Not for you, Marna."

Marna shrugged. "It will have to be."

"We'll have to see about that." She suddenly smiled as she linked her arm with Marna's. "But right now, we'll follow your Gypsy philosophy and enjoy ourselves. It's been a long time since I've been free to do that, and there's no one who knows how to do it better than the Romany."

Seven

Kira shook her head as she looked in the mirror Marna was holding before her. "Are you sure this isn't going a bit too far? I saw an old Maria Montez movie on the late-late show on television when I was in college, and even she didn't look this theatrical. *Seven* petticoats, Marna?"

"Seven is lucky." A gentle smile softened Marna's face. "You look beautiful."

Kara turned around, trying to see a back view of the outfit. There was no denying it was outrageously flattering. The full circle skirt, a pale-pink and fawn-beige print, swung gaily as she turned. It was cinched by a wide, dark brown suede belt which laced and tied in the front, reminiscent of those worn by seventeenth-century peasant women. The lace-trimmed white blouse was completely off the shoulder and made her breasts appear even more ripe and womanly. Luckily, her own calf-high brown suede boots looked good with the ensemble.

She turned back to Marna with an impish grin. "I've changed my mind. It's much more like the outfit Esmerelda wore in *The Hunchback of Notre Dame*. Are you sure you haven't hidden Quasimodo in one of the wagons?"

"Zack would not be pleased with that particular comparison," Marna said dryly. "And I wouldn't bring it up if I were you. Paulo says Zack's humor hasn't been of the best today." Her gaze narrowed curiously on Kira's face. "What did you say to him this morning?"

"Just a little misunderstanding. I'll straighten it out when I see him."

"That would be wise. I don't think many people would be comfortable having Zack 'misunderstand' them. You will be in a very vulnerable position after tonight."

She was in a very vulnerable position right now, Kira realized. What Zack thought and did and felt had already assumed monumental proportions in her life. There were moments when it frightened her. The only time she'd ever known that Zack felt a similar dependence was when he was making love to her this morning, and a sexual dependence would never be enough for her now. She mustn't borrow trouble, though, she reminded herself, because this was only the beginning. There would be time to encourage whatever he felt for her to blossom and grow into something close to the love she was feeling for him. Love. It still felt strange and new and a little intimidating. "Hadn't you better tell me what to expect during the ceremony? Will there be violins and dancing and singing?"

Marna shook her head. "This is the *mondava*. It is a very private thing. There will be just Paulo and I at the *saldana*, and then we'll leave and there will be just the two of you." Marna lowered the mirror and bent to lean it against the wheel of the wagon. "It is time. Are you ready?"

Kira drew a deep, shaky breath. She hadn't expected to be this nervous. "Yes."

The next hour was strangely hazy and remote, as if viewed in the center of a dark crystal that misted and cleared and misted again. The silent walk through the autumn woods, then her first sight of the wagon in the little glade of pines. The wagon was painted a brilliant scarlet and a campfire crackled before it, sending sparks up into the darkness.

Zack was standing in front of the wagon with an expression on his face that was more grim than serious. He was dressed in the same gray cords he had worn last night, but evidently Paulo had found him another shirt and a pair of knee-length black boots. The shirt was deep burgundy, with long full sleeves, and the rich color set off his darkness like a flame. He had left the first few buttons undone and she could see the heavy muscles that corded his chest and the beginning of the dark wedge of hair that roughened it. The cool breeze stirred the hair on his forehead, giving him the reckless and romantic appeal of Byron. Lord, he was stunning. She found herself staring up at him with the dreamy-eyed lovesickness of a teenager.

He frowned. "Why the devil are you looking at me like that? Have I grown two heads or something?"

She smiled bemusedly. "You're definitely not Quasimodo."

"What?

Marna stepped forward. "It is nothing. Kira is a bit fey tonight. Where is Paulo?"

"Here." Paulo stepped from the shadows behind the wagon. "We begin?"

Marna nodded. "We begin."

The crystal misted again as she and Zack knelt on the white sheepskin pallet before the fire. How beautiful to see things with perfect clarity and yet enhanced by this diamanté veil.

The ceremony was not long. Rich red wine was sipped from a single goblet. Marna murmured a Tamrovian blessing as she stood before them. The halves of an ancient coin that had been severed glittered in the firelight on two separate golden chains. The first talisman was slipped over Zack's head and the second around her own neck. Then Marna stepped back and there was silence for a long moment.

Kira looked up at her inquiringly. Was it over?

Marna shook her head. "Face each other and put your left hands palm to palm."

Her hand felt small and helpless as it pressed against his large palm. Fair against his darkness. Woman against man. Against? No. Merging, blending, bonding. Her startled eyes lifted to Zack's.

"Yes, I felt it too. *Mondava.*" His fingers slowly threaded through her own. "Mine."

"Mine," she repeated softly. Together. The current flowing between them was as deep and timeless as it had always been. How many times, how many moments, how many *mondavas*? It didn't matter. There was only now, only Zack looking down at her.

She was barely aware that Marna was backing away from the fire, leaving them alone in the circle of intimacy she had helped to weave about them. "Paulo," Marna prompted. Like a giant shadow, Paulo crossed to stand beside her. Kira could feel Marna's gaze on them. Love, loneliness, sadness, resignation. The emotions flowed from her in a sweeping tide that Kira felt with a poignant sensitivity she had never known before.

"Joy," Marna whispered.

The next moment Marna and Paulo were gone. The only sign of their passing was the crisp crunch of the leaves beneath their feet as they disappeared into the woods on their way back to the encampment.

Kira couldn't seem to move her gaze away from Zack's. "What are we supposed to do now?" The words were a breathless whisper.

"I think we're on our own." He smiled gently. "I know what I want to do."

"What?"

"I want to lie here beside the fire and hold you in my arms."

"That sounds like a very good idea." Each nerve and muscle in her body seemed to melt toward him. But it didn't seem all that unusual when every particle of her being was flowing into him anyway. His arms were around her and he was turning her spoon-fashion so that her head was pillowed on his arm. He hadn't released her hand and she could see their fingers still entwined in the flickering light of the fire.

His voice was low and thoughtful. "I've been in a fever for you since I left you this morning. I thought I'd be wanting you too much ever to hold you like this without making love to you."

Her eyes were fixed dreamily on the orange-gold flames of the fire. "You are making love to me."

He was silent a moment and then he kissed the tip of her ear. "Yes, I am. How perceptive of you to notice." He settled down beside her in a silence filled with companionship, beauty, and a closeness that was, at this moment, even stronger than desire. How magical to know there would still be moments like this when passion had faded.

"You're not angry with me any longer."

"I wasn't angry, I was . . ." His words trailed off. "It doesn't matter now, does it?"

No, it didn't matter now. She rubbed her cheek against the hard muscles of his arm. Contentment was a clear golden bell ringing through her—the scent of burning logs, the crisp autumn leaves, and Zack. She was perfectly relaxed but wide-awake. She had no desire to go to sleep and miss even an instant of this special time. She would lie here and enjoy the heat of the crackling fire and the warmth and security that was Zack.

"Why did you come to Tamrovia?" she asked softly. "Not this time. When you were a boy, I mean." The fire had burned low, but neither of them had wanted to stir to add another log and stoke the flames.

"I needed to get away. My grandfather had died the winter before and I had to come to terms with losing him." His lips twisted. "And I was a half-breed in a time when many southwesterners thought Indians were drunks or bums. I'd had a few experiences that year that had left me raw, and I needed to find myself. Or at least my sense of self-worth and a goal in life. I had backpacked around Italy and Switzerland for a few weeks and then crossed into Tamrovia." His gaze was fixed on the fire, but he wasn't really seeing it. "I ran into Paulo in a village in the hills and we struck up a friendship. He took me back to the encampment with him."

"And you traveled the rest of the summer with them," she finished for him. "Did you find what you were looking for?"

"Yes." His lips moved against her ear in a gossamer-light caress. "In some ways it was like being with my grandfather again. He hated to stay in one place, too, and was never happier than when he was wandering in the hills."

"Was he a hunter like you and Paulo?"

"No, he believed in being one with nature. He was a very gentle man." There was a long silence. "I loved him very much. I couldn't be like him. There was too much violence, too much hunger in me. Yet, when I was a child, I wanted to grow up to have that gentleness and serenity more than anything in the world. He was a very happy man."

And Zack hadn't been happy. The revelation was sudden, poignant for her. Understated though

Zack's admission had been, it was still painfully clear what mental and emotional hardships the little boy from two worlds had undergone. Her hand unconsciously tightened on his in silent support. "I wish I could have met your grandfather."

"He would have liked you." His eyes were suddenly twinkling. "He would have approved of your shooting pictures instead of game, even if Paulo doesn't."

"I wish I had my camera now," she said wistfully. "I could take pictures of Marna and her people here at the encampment. It would mean a good deal to her once she's left Tamrovia."

"Yes, I imagine it would. I hadn't thought of that." His arm slid around her waist. "And to you too. Did you spend much of your childhood here at the Gypsy camp?"

She shook her head. "I would have loved to have spent all of it here, but my parents and Stefan disapproved. Marna and I could escape for a full day only now and then. I loved every minute of those days. I can understand how Marna would be homesick for the life here. Do you think it would be possible for us to spend just one more day? Are they searching for us in this area?"

"I don't think so," he said slowly. "It's a little puzzling. I've been in touch with my men in Belajo and they haven't seen even a hint of pursuit. It's as if the escape had never happened. For that matter, they can't seem to get any information at all out of their informants in the palace. There appears to be a complete communication blackout."

"That's very strange, isn't it?"

He nodded. "I've told them to find out more and let me know as soon as possible."

"But you think it's safe to spend one more day here?"

"I suppose it wouldn't hurt to delay our departure until tomorrow evening instead of leaving at dawn."

"Wonderful! That will make Marna much happier."

"It will make me much happier too. I intend to be very occupied at dawn." His hand moved up to cup her breast, and she felt a ripple of sensation that shredded the fabric of tranquility she had been feeling. "In fact, I expect to be very occupied all night." His long, strong fingers probed delicately at the cotton of the blouse, circling the breast lazily. "You're not wearing anything underneath this, are you?"

"It didn't seem"—she lost words as well as breath as his thumb and forefinger plucked gently at her nipple—"appropriate."

"Oh, it wouldn't have been." His low chuckle was amused. "Nor would it have been at all efficient. You have wonderful instincts, Kira." His hand left her breast and went to her bare shoulder, rubbing the soft, silky skin lightly with the tips of his fingers. "And the loveliest shoulders I've ever seen. I have a deep admiration for both." He slid the blouse very slowly down her arm. The material tightened over her breasts and began to reveal, inch by inch, the deep cleavage. His other hand disentangled from her own and wandered to the other shoulder. He began sliding that side of the blouse down as well. She watched the material slip down with infinite slowness and knew her breasts were swelling, peaking, as if trying to burst free of the confining cloth. Excitement tautened the muscles of her stomach. Her chest was beginning to constrict and she had to breathe deeply to force oxygen into her lungs. Then her breasts broke free of the confinement of the blouse and she felt the sudden flare of sensation as her naked breasts were exposed to the heat of the fire. Her nipples were pointed and distended with arousal as her breasts jutted proudly out of the nest of cotton and lace supporting and cupping them.

Zack didn't move, but she could feel his gaze on her. She waited breathlessly. The muscles of his arm beneath her cheek were no longer relaxed, but coiled and tense. She could feel the erotic pounding of his heart against her naked back. Then his hand moved slowly up and hovered over her breast.

His fingers were long and tanned. Against the glow of the firelight they seemed to have a fiery transparency that was almost magical. Then all thought of magic vanished as his hand closed on her breast. She gasped as if she'd been kicked in the stomach. His hand was heavy and warm and very, very real as it squeezed and lifted. He played with her with a pagan, sensuous enjoyment. "Zack."

"I know," he murmured. His lips were brushing against her cheek. "I'm going crazy, too, but let's try to ease into it, love. I don't want to be as rough with you as I was this morning."

He hadn't been rough. He had been wonderful. The very violence of his passion had made it all the more intense and beautiful. She had to tell him that. "It wasn't—" She broke off as he suddenly moved away from her.

He sat up, unbuttoning his shirt, his eyes never leaving hers. "I love the way you look tonight. I like your hair tousled and wild about your shoulders." He pulled the shirt out of his trousers and slipped it off. His shoulders gleamed bronze in the firelight as he tossed the shirt away. "Sit up, Kira." He didn't wait for her to comply but pulled her gently to a sitting position. He took the bottom of her blouse and pulled it over her head and threw it on top of his shirt. Then he was tugging at her right boot. "I'm getting very proprietary about these boots," he said with a faint smile. He took the other boot off her and threw it toward the other clothing. Then he paused to gaze at her with eyes that were smoky with hunger. She could feel the tension zapping between them in jagged lines of power. "I'm beginning to feel very proprietary about you too." He moved forward and his unsteady hands untied the lace waist of her belt. When he had finished loosening the laces he hesitated, looking down at them. Then he suddenly pulled the laces so tight that her waist was cinched to wasp slimness and her naked breasts jutted forward in saucy invitation.

She gasped and her gaze flew to his. "What are you doing?"

"Fulfilling a fantasy. Hell, I didn't even know it was a fantasy until I saw you in this outfit." He kept the laces taut as he slowly lowered his head. "I'm not hurting you, am I?"

"No." His tongue was stroking her breast gently and she had trouble getting the word out. No pain, only the swollen tautness, the exquisite sensitivity of her nipples, his warm teasing tongue. The only pain was the aching desire for completion. "What fantasy?"

He released the laces, unfastened the belt, and slipped it from her waist. His eyes were darkly intent. "I don't know. It has something to do with what I felt when you walked forward into the firelight in that seventeenth-century garb." He shrugged. "*Déjà vu.* Nostalgia. Something." He unfastened his belt and pulled off his boots. "It's a night for magic and fantasy, Kira. Do you have any fantasies you want to have fulfilled?" His gaze was holding her own. "Tell me. I want to show you I can be something besides the barbarian I was this morning."

She could scarcely think, much less remember any fantasy she might have had. "I think you're doing very well on your own."

His smile was a warm flash in his dark face. "Good. Then we'll continue as we started. I'll be right back, love."

He stood and stripped quickly, then knelt beside her again. His palms framed her face and he kissed her tenderly. "Come here, Kira." His legs were spread wide and suddenly her skirt and petticoats were frothing over him. His hand was beneath them. Searching. Finding. She gasped as his fingers gently started a rhythm that caused her to clutch wildly at his shoulders. She felt the prickly abrasion of the dusting of hair on his thighs as he arranged her legs around his hips. Then his hands were on her bottom, bringing her slowly forward. She bit her lip to stifle a little moan as he began to fill the aching emptiness at an excruciatingly slow pace.

"It's like a treasure hunt, with all these petti-coats hiding you from me." He laughed huskily. "But I think I've found the way. Dear heaven, but it's a slow way."

She thought so too. "Hurry." Her nails uncon-sciously dug into the flesh of his shoulders. "This is driving me . . . crazy."

He flexed and felt a deep shudder go through her.

"Just a little more. I'm going crazy, too, but I want—" He broke off. "There. Now put your arms around me." His arms enfolded her and he buried his lips in her hair. Closeness. Fullness. Fire.

Then he was tumbling her over backward and flipping up the skirt and lace petticoats. His hand ran over her possessively. His face above her was heavy with sensuality. "Now this is the time when we hurry, Kira," he said softly. "Like this, love."

He exploded into wildness, the strokes deep and heavy with frantic urgency. She wanted to help him, but the sensations were so intense that she found she could only arch mindlessly up to him, her hands fluttering on his shoulders. Her teeth clenched as wave after wave of feeling surged over her, in her, around her. Then his lips were hard on her own as the final tidal deluge swept them away.

She couldn't move. She felt as if she might never move again. Zack's eyes were closed and his chest was rising and falling with the force of his labored breathing. There was a touch of desperation in his low laugh. "You know, another fantasy like that one might kill me. I've never felt anything so intense before." He opened his eyes and she was surprised to see how lazily sensual they were. "And do you know something else? Give me a minute or two and I'll be ready to do it again. You have a very wild effect on me, Your Highness."

"It will take me a little longer than that to recover," she murmured. "I feel as if I've just been through an earthquake."

There was a faintly regretful look in his eyes. "Pity." He slowly shifted off her. One hand moved to pet her affectionately. "I know I'm being a selfish bastard, but I can't seem to get enough of you." He unfastened her skirt, then removed both it and the petticoats. "You tell me when you're ready." He smiled crookedly. "I assure you I'm at your disposal at any time." He lay down on the sheepskin pallet and pulled her into his arms, rolling her over so they were facing each other. Then he sighed contentedly. "Though this is nice too."

"Yes." She nestled closer. "I think nice is a definite understatement." Her eyes were drooping drowsily and she smothered a yawn against his shoulder.

She was conscious of his hand running lazily down her arm to her wrist. "Take a nap, love. We have all night."

She nodded. She would sleep presently, but right now she wanted to lie here and enjoy this wonderful closeness. Then his fingers were threading once more through hers in the intimate embrace that now seemed peculiarly their own. She smiled contentedly as her heavy lids closed. The last memory of which she was conscious was the sight of their hands joined in companionship and . . .

*　　*　　*

It was early afternoon when she heard the whir of the helicopter. At first the sound was so faint it might have been the hum of a bee and she didn't bother to open her eyes. She was drowsy and content sitting here against the trunk of the beech tree, with the sun on her face and Zack's head in her lap, and it was impossible to believe anything could disturb the bucolic enchantment of the moment.

Then the chugging whir became louder and her eyes flew open. "Zack!" There was an edge of panic in her voice. "Zack, I hear something."

"Um-m," he murmured, not opening his eyes. "So do I."

"It's a helicopter." She pushed his head from her lap and jumped to her feet in a flurry of petticoats. "I'm sure it's a helicopter." She ran to the edge of the hill, her gaze searching the sky. "Zack, for God's sake, just don't lie there. They've found us!"

"I'm lying here because you nearly knocked me out when my head fell off your lap," he said dryly as he sat up.

"Oh, dear, I'm sorry." She glanced over her shoulder with a stricken expression. "But they're *here*, Zack."

A cinnamon-colored helicopter had appeared on the horizon. It was moving purposefully in their direction.

Zack rose to his feet and strolled over to stand beside her. "So I see. But the question is, Who are *they*?" He suddenly grinned down at her. "Don't worry. It's not Stefan's storm troopers. I've been expecting this particular helicopter. I radioed

Perry Bentley last night after you went to sleep and told him to fly in from Switzerland today."

"Perry Bentley?"

"My assistant. You probably saw him that night outside the theater in Tucson." He turned and started down the hill. "Put your boots on and let's go down and meet him as he lands."

She stared after him. "How did you know I was outside the theater that night?" But he was halfway down the hill and could no longer hear her. She hurriedly thrust her bare feet into the boots and tucked the tail of her blouse into her skirt. Then she was hurrying after him.

She caught up as he reached the open field. Zack's own helicopter was stashed on the perimeter, beneath the cover of overhanging trees. She watched as the aircraft landed in the exact center of the field. "How did you know I was outside—"

His hand closed on her arm as he stepped forward eagerly. "Come on. I want you to see your present." He was pulling her toward the helicopter, his expression endearingly boyish.

"My present?" she echoed bewilderedly.

The door of the helicopter was opening and the plump man who had run interference for Zack at the theater the first night she'd seen him jumped to the ground. He was dressed in casual jeans and a yellow T-shirt, and was carrying a small cardboard box.

"Perry Bentley. Kira Rubinoff." Zack introduced them absently as he took the box and handed it to Kira. "Your present."

"How do you do," Kira murmured as she opened the box. A camera. A state-of-the-art Nikon—with every conceivable lens and attachment. Her eyes lifted to Zack's. "You had him fly from Switzerland to bring me a *camera*?"

"You wanted it," he said simply. "You said it was important to you and Marna." His brow suddenly furrowed in a frown. "Don't you like it?"

She felt tears sting her eyes. What an extravagant and touching gesture! She felt a surge of feeling so intense it took her breath away. "I love it," she finally whispered huskily. Her index finger caressed the camera. "It's the most wonderful present I've ever received. Thank you, Zack."

"It's far more advanced than the first one he bought you," Bentley said cheerfully. "They've made some amazing strides in technology in the last five years. There are some instructions in the box that will show you how to use the new—" He broke off with a frown as he caught her stunned expression. "Is something wrong?"

"That's what I'm wondering," she said slowly. "But, yes, I'm beginning to think there may be something very wrong." She turned to Zack. "*You* bought me the camera Marna gave me for my eighteenth birthday?"

Zack stiffened warily. "I was going to tell you about that. Somehow I just didn't get around to it." His voice lowered. "I found myself otherwise distracted."

Her heart jerked, and for a moment the shock and bewilderment ebbed as she remembered the "distraction." Then she pulled her attention back to the subject at hand. She had an uneasy feeling this was even more important than it appeared on the surface.

She swiftly lifted her head to meet Bentley's eyes. "Zack was aware that I was outside the theater in Tucson, even though I was careful to keep in the background. Now how do you suppose he knew, Mr. Bentley?"

Bentley cast an uncomfortable glance at Zack. Then, when his employer slowly nodded permission, he said, "The security man who was tailing you called me on the car phone."

"*Tailing* me? What security man?"

"The one who has been assigned to protect you for the last seven years," Bentley said. He was definitely uneasy now and his words came out choppily. "Jansen is one of Mr. Damon's best security men."

Kira felt as if she were lost in a maze of mirrors where nothing appeared as it really was. "Seven years?"

"Actually, it was more like ten," Zack said quietly. "I became very dissatisfied with Stefan's slipshod security and decided to protect you myself." He motioned with a jerk of his thumb. "The encampment is through that grove of poplars, Perry. Please go wait for us there."

"Right," Bentley said in evident relief before he scurried toward the stand of trees.

"I think you owe me an explanation," Kira said carefully.

He nodded. "Yes, I think I do too. I first heard about you the summer I was nineteen. Marna had come to the camp to nurse her mother and I was always off in the hills with Paulo so I didn't see much of her at first. Then I began to catch her staring at me." He smiled crookedly. "Rather like a housewife considering the merits of a piece of meat for a stew. One day she took me aside and told me about the *mondava*. She also told me about a child called Kira, who was the other half of me. She said that one day, after the child had become a woman, she would send her to me." He paused. "I didn't believe a word of it. I was accustomed to a certain amount of mysticism, but mysticism is difficult to accept when applied to one's own self. The whole thing sounded like a soap opera or one of those old bodice-ripper novels. A royal princess couldn't be the other half of a half-breed like Zack Damon. Not in real life. So I went back to Arizona and began to dismiss it from my mind." He slowly shook his head. "I didn't take Marna's determination into account. The first letter came a month later."

"Letter?"

"She wrote me every month or so. I was moving around a great deal then and I don't know how she managed to keep track of me, but somehow she did." His eyes met hers. "They were always about you. What you'd said and what you'd done. Occasionally she'd send me a snapshot or a hair ribbon or a page of your homework on which you'd gotten a particularly good grade. I gradually got to know you. I looked forward to those letters as if you were *my* child. Then, as you grew older, that feeling began to change. You were still mine, but not *enough* mine. I began to think about the *mondava* and to believe in it." His voice dropped to a whisper. "I was growing very impatient by the time Marna sent you to me in Tucson. I don't think I could have waited much longer before I came to you. Perhaps Marna knew that."

"She probably did." Kira ran her fingers distract-edly through her hair. "And she certainly wouldn't have wanted her precious *mondava* to be spoiled. There's more, isn't there? Marna's rescue was a lit-tle too smooth to have been effected on the spur of the moment. You already knew she was being held prisoner when I came to you."

Zack nodded. "The bribe had been arranged over a month ago. I had a special operative, Steve Dubliss, waiting in Switzerland. We were planning to go in after her in the next few days."

She shook her head in bewilderment. "You and Marna seem to have planned everything, down to the last detail." She whirled away from him. "I've just thought of something. I don't believe you've told me the whole story. I have to talk to Marna."

He fell into step with her as she hurried toward the encampment. "It's not as if we were trying to hurt you," he said gently. "Why are you so upset, Kira?"

"I can't talk about it now," she said jerkily. "I have to talk to Marna. I have to know everything."

He opened his mouth to speak and then closed it again. He was silent the rest of the way.

Marna was standing on the edge of the little crowd surrounding Perry Bentley, but she broke away as she caught sight of Kira and Zack. She came toward them with a wide smile on her face. "A camera, Kira. How you will love—" She broke off as she caught sight of Kira's tense expression. "What is wrong?"

"She knows everything, Marna," Zack said with a rueful shrug.

"Not quite everything," Kira snapped. "But I'm

beginning to suspect quite a lot." She drew a deep breath. "Marna, when we crossed the border back into Tamrovia from Sedikhan and arrived at the Gypsy camp, how did Stefan's soldiers know we'd show up there?"

Marna gazed at her impassively for a long moment. "I told Paulo to send an anonymous message to Stefan telling him when we'd arrive."

Zack let his breath out in a low whistle. "I didn't know that. Do you suppose Machiavelli had any Gypsy blood?"

Marna shrugged. "If he had been Gypsy, he would have had the sense not to become involved in all those intrigues and enjoyed his life instead. Intrigue should be used only infrequently to accomplish one's ends."

"You *deceived* me," Kira said in disbelief. "I was so frightened and worried about you, and it was you who deliberately arranged for your own capture. Why, Marna, why?"

"It was time for the *mondava*," Marna said simply. "I had to find a way to send you to Zack and set it into motion."

"She only did it for your happiness, Kira," Zack said quietly.

"I know that." Kira's voice was charged with tension. "She'd walk through fire to make sure I was happy."

Marna nodded. "It was for the best."

"You're both being so marvelously soothing and unconcerned about it all." Kira's sapphire eyes were suddenly blazing in her pale face. "Don't you realize what you've done? You've *manipulated* me! All my life I've been just a chess piece for Stefan and my parents to move around the chessboard. I accepted that." Her smile was bittersweet. "Perhaps not tamely, but I could accept it because they didn't really care about me. But you love me, Marna, and yet you've manipulated me too." She turned to Zack. "And didn't it ever occur to you to come to me in all those years and not wait for Marna to pull the strings? You know, I don't think it did. I was just an empty-headed doll to you. Well, I'm *not* a chess piece or a puppet or a doll. I'm none of those things, and I'm not a child, either."

Zack took an impulsive step toward her. "Kira—"

"No." She backed away from him. "Don't touch me. I can't think when you touch me. And it's time I stopped reacting and started thinking."

"You are hurting." There was a flicker of sadness in Marna's face. "I never meant for you to experience pain."

"Perhaps it's time I did experience pain," Kira said huskily. "Whenever I was with you, Marna, I felt I had stepped out of the glass bubble. But I hadn't, not really. A strong, overprotective love can be just as effective in keeping someone from the real world as protocol and a ring of guards." She thrust the box with the camera in it at Marna. "Will you keep this for me? I have some thinking to do and I want to go back up on the hill to do it."

"I'd like to come with you," Zack said.

She shook her head. "I want to be alone." She smiled shakily. "You distract me too. I'll try not to be long." She started away and then turned back to them. "It's not that I don't know how good you've both been to me. It's just that I feel as I did the other night when Paulo ruffled my hair and called

me a child. I can't let that . . ." She made a helpless
little movement with one hand and turned away
again. "I'll be back soon."

It was dusk when Kira came down from the hill.
She had watched the piercing blue of the sky turn
to the blazing scarlet of sunset and then fade to the
gentle violet of twilight. She had felt the warmth of
the Indian summer afternoon cool to autumn
evening chill, and still she had sat under the beech
tree lost in thought.

Zack and Marna were alone at the *saldana* when
she walked into camp. The evening campfire had
been lit and the pungent smell of coffee drifted to
her.

Marna glanced up from her cup. "You haven't
had anything to eat since lunch. I've made a stew."

"I'm not hungry. I'll take some coffee, though,"
Kira said as she strolled over to the fire and plopped
down on the sheepskin pallet beside Zack. She
crossed her legs tailor-fashion and took the tin cup
Marna handed her. Marna returned to her stool on
the other side of the fire and picked up her own cup
again.

Kira felt their concern as she took a sip of the
strong, hot coffee and looked up with a half-
comical grimace. "I feel like Moses coming down
from the mountain with the ten commandments. I
didn't mean to be that pretentious when I stalked
off. I haven't made any philosophical discoveries
that will shake the world." She paused. "Except
perhaps my own."

"And ours," Zack said quietly. "Everything you

do and say and think are very important to us. Did it help, Kira?"

"Yes, it did help." She cradled her cup in her hands as she gazed into the fire. "For one thing, I decided I had no right to be upset with either one of you. If you manipulated me, it was because I let myself be manipulated. I've made a habit of acting impulsively. I relied on you, Marna, to do my thinking." She met Marna's gaze across the campfire. "No mature adult would let herself be sent to a stranger with instructions 'to do whatever was necessary.' I was so accustomed to relying on you and believing you were always right that I merely followed your instructions without questioning them." She held up her hand as Marna would have interrupted. "I don't say that I wouldn't have done it if I'd stopped to consider. There's a good chance I would have acted in exactly the way I did. But I would have known it was my choice, the choice of an independent individual." She paused as if searching for words. "You see, I've always played at being independent with my little defiances, but I've never been willing to take that extra step into true independence." She laughed shakily. "I was frightened, I guess. As long as I was an irresponsible child I didn't have to commit myself totally to anything or anyone. Well, I've decided I can't live that way anymore. I have to assume the responsibilities that go along with love."

She set her cup down and spread her hands on her knees, her fingers flexing nervously. She drew a deep breath. "I love you, Marna, and I'm going to keep on loving you until the day I die. You're going to be a part of me for the rest of my life. I don't give a damn what you think the *mondava* is going to do to our relationship. I *know* myself and I know my love for you isn't going to change . . . except to grow stronger maybe." She turned to Zack. "And I love you too. I've never told you before. We've all been so concerned with this *mondava* business that we've ignored the basics."

Zack smiled faintly. "I'd say you couldn't get much more basic than the *mondava*."

She met his eyes directly. "Yes, you could. There's always a plain old-fashioned declaration of undying devotion. Which you haven't made, by the way. I think there are several people around here besides me who have a few problems." She made an impatient gesture with one hand. "We'll address that later. Right now, I just want you to know I love you. And no matter how you feel about me at the moment, someday I'm going to know that you love me too. You once said I had the idea my value lay only in my title, and maybe you were right. But I've been thinking about it, and I'm a hell of a lot more than a title. I have intelligence and stamina and determination."

"And a very loving heart," Zack said softly. "Thank God."

Her eyes met his with glowing serenity. "Oh, yes, I have that too. Any man who gets me will have a prize. I'm going to make sure you appreciate me, Zack." She was having trouble tearing her gaze away. His dark eyes reflected so many wonderful things—pride, understanding, tenderness. She finally managed it and looked back into the flames. "However, that's all going to have to wait. I'm going to have to straighten out this mess with Stefan before I'm free to pursue you."

Zack stiffened warily. "I don't like the sound of that."

"I didn't think you would." She made a face. "You're going to like even less the way I intend doing it. I'm going to fly back to the palace tonight and make Stefan give me his word that Marna will be allowed either to live with or visit her tribe without any interference on his part."

"No!" Marna said harshly, coming erect on her stool.

"Yes," Kira said firmly. "I'm not going to let you suffer for helping me. Stefan was wrong. I just can't cave in on something this important."

"You tried to convince him before." Zack's face reflected none of the resistance she had expected. His expression was merely speculative. "What makes you think you can do it now, when you couldn't do it then?"

"I pleaded. I appealed. I reasoned. Now I'm going to try something else. I'm going to set forth my terms and cram them down his throat. If I'm forced to, I'll blackmail him. I'll tell him I'll give interviews to the press revealing conditions in Tamrovia. I'll even involve Sedikhan if there's absolutely no other way. If you decide to do something, it's worth going all the way." Her lips curved in a tiny smile. "Or so someone told me quite recently."

"You're not going back to the palace. I fight my own battles." Marna's eyes were flashing.

"This isn't one of your battles. It's mine," Kira said just as firmly. "And make up your mind that I'm going to be the one to fight it."

Zack set his cup on the ground. "All right. We go back to the palace tonight." He ignored Marna's low cry of protest. "I'm not sure what good it will do, but we'll give it a try."

Kira shook her head. "No, not 'we.' Me. I'm going back alone."

Zack didn't reply for a moment. "I rather thought you had something of the sort in mind."

"I wouldn't be the one fighting the battle if I had Zack Damon beside me, ready to exert economic and political muscle." She shook her head. "I'll do this my way."

His expression was inscrutable as he studied her face for a long moment. "Okay." He rose abruptly to his feet. "You return by yourself. I'll go get Paulo and we'll pull the helicopter out from under the tree cover and check it out. You'd better change your clothes." He smiled. "As beautiful as you look, that's not an outfit in which to discuss ultimatums. It's entirely too soft and feminine."

Kira was startled that he'd given in so easily. She stood up, her eyes narrowed on him with a touch of suspicion. "No arguments?"

He shook his head. "It's your battle." He looked toward Marna. "And your debt. I respect that. I'll meet you in the clearing in fifteen minutes."

Marna was glowering ferociously at both of them. "I've changed my mind. You are a *chitka*, Zack. Tell her not to go. You are joined in the *mondava*. She will listen to you."

"If she did listen, she'd be taking a step backward. I wouldn't ask her to do that." He turned away. "Fifteen minutes."

Eight

Full darkness had fallen by the time Kira had
changed back into her jeans, sweater, and jacket
and walked the short distance through the woods
to the clearing. The helicopter had already been
moved out into the open by Zack, Paulo, and
Bentley, who were waiting beside it. Marna stood
apart, holding a lantern, whose glow revealed the
grimness of her expression.

Kira crossed to her at once and stood on tiptoe to
plant a kiss on her broad jaw. "It would make me
feel a good deal better if you'd wish me well."

"Why should I wish you well when you're doing a
chitka thing like—" She broke off, a multitude of
conflicting emotions crossing her face. "Good journey," she said gruffly. "Better than you deserve."
She enfolded Kira in a breathtaking bear hug.
"And if Stefan causes you problems, I will make a

spell that will cause his *nudocs* to rot and fall off. I'm very weary of his stupidity." She released Kira and gave her a gentle whack on the derriere. "Go."

Kira's eyes were misty as she covered the few yards to where Zack was standing by the helicopter. Perry Bentley had left the clearing and Paulo had taken a few steps back to allow them a limited amount of privacy.

"I'd be interested in knowing if those *nudocs* that are about to be cursed are what I think they are," Zack murmured as he opened the door of the helicopter.

"To put it delicately, *nudocs* are a gentleman's private parts," Kira said with a grin.

Zack flinched. "Hm-m. So I thought. I'll be very careful not to risk incurring that particular curse." His gaze was suddenly grave. "Are you going to tell me what your plans are?"

"I'm just going to talk to Stefan. I'll land the helicopter in the clearing in the woods across from the main gate and go through the cave and the secret tunnel into the palace itself." She shrugged. "I could just march in through the front gate, but I'd prefer to take him off guard. It's likely that I'm going to need every advantage I can manage. When I succeed in bringing Stefan around to my way of thinking, I'll contact you by radio."

"*When*, not *if*?" Zack asked with a slight smile. "You're very confident."

She drew a quivering breath. "I can't let myself be anything else. Otherwise, I'd be shaking like a bowl full of jelly."

"I don't think so. I'd bet your brother Lance would say his little sister had definitely 'set.' " He suddenly crushed her in his arms and kissed her with a hard, bruising passion that robbed her of breath and made her head whirl. He lifted his head and glared down at her fiercely. "Be careful, dammit. And stay away from Karpathan!"

"I will," she promised a little dazedly.

Then he lifted her into the helicopter and closed the door behind her. She watched him step back beside Paulo as she turned on the ignition. Zack looked strong and powerful and able to take on the world, and, for an instant, she was almost tempted to let him come with her. It would be very comforting to lean on his strength. Oh, Lord, she was doing it again. It was clearly going to take practice to get her thinking into the right groove; she wouldn't lean on anyone. Not anymore. She waved and lifted off. Soon the figures in the clearing had vanished from view and only the light of the lantern Marna was holding remained visible. Then, as she turned south, the light, too, disappeared.

"I didn't think you would let her go," Paulo said with a sidewise glance at Zack's tense, set face. "Until the very last minute I thought you'd change your mind and either make her stay or go with her."

"A time to set free." Zack's eyes were still on the horizon where the lights from the helicopter had just vanished. "It was time to set her free to be her own person."

Paulo nodded slowly. "It was a wise move. Now she'll return to you and be your person as well."

"Dear Lord, I hope so." Zack suddenly realized

his hands were clenched. He carefully relaxed them. He needed patience and control now more than at any time in his life, and he had to concentrate on gathering those forces to him. It had nearly ripped him apart to stand and watch her take off in the helicopter. She had looked so damned *alone*. "Let's go back to the *saldana*. I told Perry to contact my men in Belajo by radio to be on the lookout for her. I want to see if they've heard any more from the palace." He glanced around. "Where's Marna?"

Paulo shrugged as he fell into step with Zack. "She probably wanted to be alone. She does not like this."

"Who the hell does?" Zack growled. "It's tearing my guts out. The only thing giving me any comfort at all is that I know, as autocratic as Stefan may be, he's not likely to imprison his own sister."

"You would have to argue with Marna there," Paulo said dryly. "She thinks he's capable of every stupid action imaginable."

"You're not very reassuring."

"Realities must be faced." Paulo's eyes narrowed speculatively on Zack's face. "What would you do if he did decide to do that?"

"I'd go in and get her," Zack said grimly. "And on the way I'd flex enough economic muscle to topple King Stefan from his throne. Then I'd make sure that Marna didn't have to put a curse on Stefan's *nudocs*. I'd rip them off myself."

Paulo laughed softly. "Well, it's nice to know you have an alternative plan. I do like a man who thinks ahead." They had arrived at the *saldana*, and Paulo paused by the fire to clap him on the shoulder. "We didn't finish that bottle the other night. Shall we try again? I think you have more to forget tonight than you did then."

"There may be a problem, Zack." Perry Bentley had emerged from the caravan and was climbing down to the ground. "There's something funny going on in Belajo."

Zack became very still. "What do you mean 'funny'?"

Perry shifted his shoulders uneasily, "You know Fontaine hasn't been able to get any word from his people in the palace. Well, he sent a few men to nose around to see what they could find out." He hesitated. "Something weird is happening there. No one goes in. No one goes out. And there's a cordon of soldiers around the palace. Not palace guards, regular soldiers."

Zack muttered a violent curse. "A coup?"

Perry shook his head. "I don't know. Maybe."

"Not a coup," Paulo said slowly. "A revolution, I think."

Zack glanced at him sharply. "You know something?"

"It fits together. That strange new prey I mentioned moving around in the hills? Bands of men. *Large* bands of men."

"Guerillas," Zack muttered. "Damn, why did you keep all this to yourself?"

"They left me alone. I left them alone." Paulo shrugged. "I did liberate a few of their weapons. They are in my wagon at the encampment if you'd like to see them. They are very high powered." He paused. "And Russian-made."

"Get them," Zack said tersely. "We may need them."

Paulo's wide smile shone with feral pleasure. "We are going hunting?"

"We're going hunting," Zack confirmed grimly. "Perry, radio Fontaine and tell him to get together enough men for a small force and meet us in the woods south of the main gate. But before you do that, try to raise Kira on the helicopter radio and warn her." He looked at his wristwatch. "I doubt if you'll be able to do it. She should have landed a few minutes ago. Try anyway."

"Right." Perry jumped up to the wagon seat and disappeared into the caravan.

Paulo raised his brows. "So much for setting the little one free."

"I set her free to walk right into a damn revolution." Zack's voice held an edge of agonized desperation. "I should have gone with her. God knows what she's going to run into once she reaches the palace." He turned with barely concealed violence. "Get those weapons. I'll meet you at Perry's helicopter."

The soldier's hands were rough as he pushed her into Stefan's library. Kira's eyes were shooting sparks and she murmured something a trifle off-color as she watched the door swing shut behind him. "Stefan, what's going on here? There are soldiers all over the palace and that idiot was actually rough as hell with—" She broke off as the tall, shadowy figure stepped out of the dimness by the bookshelves into the shallow pool of light formed by the desk lamp. "Sandor! I told that soldier I wanted to see Stefan."

"So he told me," Karpathan said wearily. "Kira, what the devil are you doing back here? I thought you'd be out of the country by now." He dropped down into Stefan's oversized executive chair. "And how did you get in without coming through the main gate?"

"That's none of your business, Sandor. Where is my brother? I came to see Stefan."

"Stefan is safe. Which is more than I can say for you. Everyone in the palace must know you've returned by now."

"Safe? Why shouldn't I be safe? This is all very irregular, Sandor."

"Revolution has a way of being irregular," Karpathan said dryly.

"Revol—" Kira's eyes widened in shock. She felt a wave of panic wash over her. "Where is Stefan?"

"That's what we'd like to know," a deep baritone voice said from behind her. "He's been most elusive, hasn't he, Sandor?"

She turned to face the short, bull-chested man who had entered the library. There was no question of not recognizing him. That strong, deeply grooved face was completely unforgettable. "Naldona!"

He smiled a trifle unpleasantly. "I don't believe we were introduced at that meeting two years ago, but I recognize you as well. Your photograph caused me a good deal of trouble, Your Highness."

"It merely escalated your plans," Karpathan said smoothly as he rose to his feet. "It may even have helped your cause by creating a martyr image."

Marc Naldona strolled forward to stand beside Karpathan. "It's very difficult to remember that, when I recall how uncomfortable I was hiding in the hills those first few weeks."

"I didn't mean to hurt you," Kira whispered. "I only wanted to help. I admired you very much, Mr. Naldona."

"Well, it's fortunate that I'm going to be able to give you the opportunity to make amends." His smile was hard and slightly menacing. "We're going to make good use of you."

Kira shivered. The whole episode was wildly unbelievable and everything was topsy-turvy. Nothing was as she had thought it was. Even the two men facing her appeared to have changed places in some subtle manner. Naldona, whom she had only seen in rough work clothes and who had always seemed totally of the earth and the people, was faultlessly dressed in an expensive-looking, dark blue business suit. Karpathan, on the other hand, had shed his fastidious elegance and was dressed with utmost simplicity in black jeans and a long-sleeved black shirt. It should have detracted from his forceful presence but somehow only served to magnify it. That force was charging the room with electricity at the moment. There was an air of antagonism between the two men that was nearly tangible. She felt as if she had been thrown into a cage with two rogue tigers and couldn't be sure if they were going to rend her or each other.

She lifted her chin. "I object to being used by anyone, Mr. Naldona. I think you'll find it's more bother than it's worth to try to force me to do anything."

"You're very brave," Naldona said silkily. "Perhaps you think that because your brother indulged your little pranks, we will do the same? We will use you as we please. I think a princess might do as well as a king under the circumstances, don't you, Sandor?"

"You know what I think," Karpathan said curtly. "It's the height of madness. You can't get away with that kind of barbarism today. We're not in czarist Russia and she's not a Romanov."

"But an example *is* needed to make the world take us seriously." Naldona's dark eyes were burning feverishly in his hollow-cheeked face.

"That was Idi Amin's philosophy and I can't see that he earned any great amount of respect or admiration," Karpathan said dryly. "Butchery seldom earns you anything but an eventual one-way ticket out of power."

Butchery. Romanovs. Kira felt the blood freeze in her veins. They were talking about assassination. "Murder," she whispered.

"Justice," Naldona corrected.

She shook her head. "Stefan may have been guilty of oppression and of allowing certain inequities, but he wasn't a murderer."

"Autocrats like your brother murder hope and initiative among the people," Naldona snapped. "It can amount to the same thing."

"An action like the one you're contemplating would foster sympathy and support for Stefan from countries outside Tamrovia," Karpathan said. "We don't want that."

"Not if it's handled correctly." Naldona shrugged. "A mob is the easiest thing in the world to arouse if one knows how to go about it. Then we'd only be guilty of not being able to protect her from the righteous wrath of the people."

"No," Karpathan said flatly.

Kira felt a surge of relief that made her knees weak.

Naldona's eyes narrowed on Karpathan's face. "You forget you're no longer in control here, Sandor. You've proved very helpful, but don't push me."

Karpathan's expression was inscrutable as he met Naldona's gaze. Then he glanced away. "It's not worth quarreling about. Do as you wish."

Murder her he meant, Kira thought with sick horror. So casual. Her death wasn't worth bothering about. "You're both monsters."

Naldona's smile was almost cheerful. "It's all in the perspective. To some, we'll be known as the saviors of our country." He started across the room toward the door. "She'll have to be transferred from the palace to a more accessible spot. It mustn't look as if we have any direct connection with this. It will just be a spontaneous outpouring of national feeling. I'll call the guard."

"You do that," Karpathan murmured lazily. He was moving around the desk toward Naldona with the swift, silent stealth of a panther.

"I'm glad you're being reasonable," Naldona was saying as he reached for the knob of the door. "We have to stand together on all things, Sandor. Once you've thought about it, I'm sure—"

Karpathan's karate chop to the back of Naldona's neck dropped him like a stone. Kira watched numbly as he fell heavily to the Aubusson carpet. It was no more astounding than anything else that had happened since she had opened the door of her suite to find the hall crowded with soldiers.

"Don't just stand there," Karpathan said harshly as he took her elbow and pushed her toward the door. "He's not dead and he won't be unconscious indefinitely. Do you like the idea of being torn apart by a mob? Naldona has the rhetorical skill of a fallen angel, if you remember."

"I remember." She shook her head to clear it. "But why should I trust you any more than I do him? It's clear you're in this plot as deeply as your friend here."

"He's not my friend. There was a time when I thought he might become one, but . . ." Karpathan shrugged. "Water under the bridge. He doesn't want the same things I do for Tamrovia and we've come to a parting of the ways. I assure you that you're far safer with me than with him."

"Really? You played Judas to Stefan, and I haven't the slightest doubt you masterminded this revolution."

He bowed mockingly. "Thank you for your faith in my intellectual capability. I did mastermind it, as a matter of fact." His glance was suddenly razor sharp. "As for playing Judas, I'd do it again if I thought it was necessary. I did think there was a chance I'd be able to manipulate Stefan into effecting radical enough changes so that all this might not have had to become a reality. Unfortunately, it was taking too long for Naldona to tolerate." His face became somber. "Naldona's not the man I thought he was. If I let him take control now, it would mean a reign of terror."

"Why would he want—"

"Look, we don't have time for this. I'd very much like to get you out of here with your skin intact, but unless we hurry, it might not be possible." His eyes glittered fiercely. "Yes, I'm a revolutionary and I'm going to do everything in my power to make this country a republic. However, I'm neither a warmonger nor a Marxist, and Naldona is both, as I've only recently discovered." As he met her still suspicious gaze the fierceness faded and weariness replaced it. "Kira, I like you. I've always liked you. I've even tried to help you whenever possible. Who do you think persuaded Stefan to give Marna quarters in the palace instead of imprisoning her?"

"Yet you were going to have her transferred to the prison. Stefan told me you'd convinced him to do it, the night we escaped."

He shook his head. "I knew you'd come back to help her escape. Her guards were in my pay. When Damon's men offered them a bribe they came to me." He paused. "I told them to take it. Time was running out, though, and I had to get you to move fast. You had to be out of the palace by the time Naldona arrived. I was to cut all the communication lines and take over the palace the night of the reception. It wasn't until after I had made the suggestion to Stefan about transferring Marna that one of the guards came to me and told me you'd already made plans to free her during the reception." He suddenly smiled with beguiling warmth.

"It was a brilliant escape, by the way. It was as if you'd faded into the woodwork."

Kira felt an answering smile tug at her lips. "In a manner of speaking, that was what we did . . . Sandor."

"Ah, a break in the wall of your suspicion at last," he said with a sigh of relief. "Now, if you'll just cooperate a little further and tell me how you manage to get in and out of the palace without being seen, we just might get out of here alive, sweet cousin."

She hesitated and then said slowly, "There's a secret passage in my suite that leads under the front gate about a quarter of a mile into the woods and exits into a small cave."

"Good! Then we may have a chance." He cast a quick glance at Naldona. "He's still not stirring." His hand tightened on her elbow. "You're my prisoner, understand? Most of these soldiers are men Naldona brought with him from his base and they won't take my orders. Naldona has made sure there won't be any division of loyalty in his personal aides." He opened the door. "Try to look frightened and properly chastened, will you? It will be expected."

"That won't be a chore," Kira said ruefully. "My knees haven't stopped shaking since I stepped into this room."

"I wouldn't have known it," he said with surprising gentleness. "You're a very brave lady, Kira."

Then, as he saw the soldier standing guard across the hall come to attention, his face set in harsh lines. He pushed her roughly out into the hall. "Straight ahead, and don't try anything stupid, bitch. It would give me great pleasure to stop any attempt at escape in the most painful way possible."

Nine

Kira drew a breath of relief as the door of her suite closed behind them. The halls had been crowded with soldiers and every second she had expected to hear a shout behind them signaling that Naldona had regained consciousness and given the alarm.

"It's over here." She ran across to the bookcase and turned the candelabra on the wall beside it. The bookcase began to open slowly.

"Interesting," Sandor said as he joined her. "My home in Limtana has a secret passage too. Useful little additions, aren't they?" His glance traveled to the photograph of Naldona on the wall. "So that's the picture that caused all the uproar. I've never seen it before. I was out of the country when Naldona took to the hills."

"I still can't believe what he's become." Kira took

a pen flashlight out of her pocket and flicked it on. "I thought he was so sincere."

"So did I." There was profound regret in Sandor's voice. "Perhaps he was at one time. Power has a habit of corrupting even the most idealistic of men." He followed her into the passage and waited while she closed off the entrance. "So now, instead of having an absolute monarchy, we're going to have an absolute dictatorship." His lips tightened grimly. "Until I can find a way of ousting him."

"Can you do that?"

"I *have* to do it. He couldn't have grown this powerful without my help. I'm the one who created our Frankenstein and brought all this down on Tamrovia." His eyes darkened. "But whatever happens, the monarchy is gone forever. You have to understand that. It was a dinosaur and the time had come for it to pass into oblivion."

"I've realized that for a long time." A tiny smile curved Kira's lips. "Did you think I'd be outraged that Stefan and I are out of jobs?"

"Not really." He returned her smile with a warmth that startled her as he followed her down the steps. "I had an idea you were a republican at heart. It made it very difficult playing the rascally villain around you."

"It didn't appear to cause you undue strain," Kira said, casting him a grin over her shoulder. "You did it exceptionally well. You evidently have a certain flare for it."

"Ouch," he said, flinching. "I believe I've been stung. That was most uncousinly, Ki— What the hell is that?"

His voice was so intense that Kira's gaze flew to follow his into the darkness ahead. There was a bobbing light moving swiftly toward them through the passage.

Kira inhaled sharply. "Someone must have discovered the opening in the cave."

"It's possible," Sandor said slowly. "Naldona's forces are all over the grounds. It's either that or one of our illustrious ancestors returning to haunt the hallowed halls."

How could he be so cool? She laughed shakily. "If it is, I'm probably safe. It's you who's just dethroned the Rubinoffs."

"You'll be safe, anyway." He stepped ahead of her in the passageway. "Or as safe as I can keep you. God, I hope there aren't too many of them."

The beam was much closer now and she could see Sandor's wide shoulders tense beneath the black shirt. She was having trouble breathing. The walls were closing in on her in the narrow passage. Rats in a trap, she thought wildly. Caught like rats in a trap.

Abruptly the light ahead stopped as it splayed out to reveal Sandor blocking the passageway. There was an instant of silence that lasted at least a thousand years.

"Stand aside, Karpathan, or we'll blow you out of the way."

Zack's voice!

Her heart zoomed to her throat and she ducked around Sandor and ran the intervening yards separating them. "Zack, it's all right! It's me." She was in his arms, hugging him with such strength that he gasped in surprise.

Then she heard him chuckle as his arms closed around her. "Remind me to teach you battlefield etiquette sometime. One of the most explicit rules is: When threatened with being blown apart, do not make a dash and throw yourself into your adversary's arms. Very bad form."

"Is it?" He was so big and secure and wonderfully, marvelously *here.* "But you weren't threatening me, you were threatening Sandor."

"In this darkness I might have had trouble telling you apart." He suddenly stiffened and his gaze lifted from her face to fasten on Sandor. "Don't move, Karpathan. Paulo still has you covered. Did he hurt you, Kira?"

"No, of course not. Naldona wanted to make a Romanov of me. Sandor actually saved my life."

"Which act may prove futile if we don't postpone these explanations and get out of here," Sandor said impatiently. "It's likely Naldona has already given the alarm and they're combing the area for miles around."

Zack glanced down at Kira. "Was Karpathan in the conspiracy?"

"Yes, but it's not—" Kira stopped. "I trust him, Zack. We haven't time for anything else. Naldona wants my head in a basket." She smiled with an effort. "And, as I'm not at all sure I could be as dignified as Marie Antoinette at the guillotine, I think we'd better try to avoid it."

"We will," Zack said quietly. He released Kira and made a motion with the flashlight in his hand. "Okay, Karpathan, we'll trust you. But if you try to lead us into a trap, I promise you that it will be *your* head in the basket." He turned. "Let's go!" He took off at a brisk trot, with the rest of them following close behind.

As Kira fell into pace beside Paulo she glanced curiously at the long, snout-nosed weapon he was carrying. "What a weird-looking gun. Was that what you were going to blast us with, Paulo?"

He nodded. "It would have been quite a blast," he said cheerfully. "It's a flamethrower."

Her eyes widened. "You go hunting with a flamethrower?"

"No, *his* friends go hunting with flame-throwers." Paulo's head jerked back to indicate Sandor. "Isn't that right, Karpathan?"

"You've run into my men in the hills," Sandor said grimly. "I'll tear a strip off them for losing those weapons."

"They didn't lose them. I confiscated them. They're not bad, those soldiers of yours. Very quiet, very fast, very disciplined." He grinned. "Too bad they are not Gypsies. Then they would be perfect."

They reached the rear of the cave and Zack slipped through the twisting, narrow opening that was hidden by an overhanging rock. "It's all right," he called. "The cave's empty." He was striding quickly toward the front entrance. "I left Perry, Fontaine, and four men standing guard at Perry's helicopter a short distance from here, but I noticed you landed closer, Kira. We'll use that one. I'll tell Fontaine to get his men into the helicopter and prepare to take off. I'll be right back."

Five minutes later Kira was at the controls of the helicopter and Paulo and Sandor were seated and ready to take off. She had started the engine and the rotors were whirring, but there was still no Zack.

"There has to be trouble. Surely he should be back by now." Kira's hand tightened on the stick as cold terror shook her. "I'm going after him."

"I'll go." Sandor opened the door of the helicopter.

Shots! A deadly rat-a-tat from the direction of the woods into which Zack had disappeared.

Paulo muttered a low curse and jumped to the ground, the flamethrower ready in his hands.

Then Kira saw Perry's helicopter suddenly rise sluggishly above the trees, gaining altitude with reckless swiftness. The gunfire escalated in intensity.

"The soldiers must have heard their helicopter and closed in just before it took off," Sandor said. "That means they'll be streaming all over the place in a second. Where the hell is Damon?"

Oh, dear God, she prayed, don't let him get shot. She wouldn't be able to bear it if anything happened to Zack. "Well, I'm not going to wait any longer to find out. I'm going after him." Her voice was tense and ragged as she fumbled at the handle of the door. "I won't let him stay out there alone. They're *shooting*, dammit."

The shots were coming closer. She suddenly saw Zack break clear of the shrubbery at the edge of the clearing and streak toward them! He wasn't hurt. She was so relieved that she felt a little dizzy.

"How close are they?" Paulo shouted.

"Too close," Zack said curtly. "An entire company of them. They're right on my heels."

Paulo's grin glittered in the darkness. "Well, let us see if we can't discourage them."

He lifted the flamethrower and swept it in a wide arc across the shrubs and the trees that bordered the clearing, and then brought it back again. A whoosh, an explosion, and then the woods were aflame! The flames curled and soared, forming a wall of fire that writhed as if it were a living entity in the darkness. Kira could hear startled voices shouting in frustration beyond that barrier of flame.

"Let's see them get through that," Paulo said with satisfaction as he shouldered the weapon.

"I'm glad you didn't become trigger-happy in that passage," Sandor said dryly. "That's a very effective weapon."

"Too easy," Paulo said with a shrug. "No challenge. Anyone can win with this." He turned to Zack, who was now climbing into the helicopter. "Isn't that right, Zack? Besides, who wants to destroy all those beautiful trees?"

"Get into the helicopter, Paulo. Sorry there's no more fun to be had tonight. Lift off, Kira." Zack dropped into the seat beside her. His hand covered Kira's on the stick. "Are you all right?"

Was *she* all right? He was the one who had been dodging bullets. She nodded jerkily. "I will be as soon as we get out of here." The helicopter lifted, hovered, and then straightened out as it gained altitude. There was a sudden barrage of artillery fire as the helicopter became visible over the flames, but then they were out of range.

"Where are we going?" she asked, glancing at Zack.

"The encampment, first. We'll just have to take one thing at a time."

She nodded and turned the helicopter toward the north. She could still see the spiraling clouds of black smoke and the blazing inferno of the woods below. It was a macabre contrast to the gently winking lights of the turreted palace that had once been her home. Then she could no longer see either the woods or the palace as the helicopter sped out of Belajo toward safety.

When they landed in the glade at the encampment, the brilliant beams of the helicopter lights revealed Marna standing patiently, her head thrown back, looking up at them.

Paulo jumped out as soon as the ignition was turned off. "I will go and explain matters and try to smooth the path. Marna will not be pleased that you let Kira walk into that situation at the palace, Zack."

"Let?" Kira asked pointedly.

Zack smiled. "Sorry, love, no offense meant. We know that it would have taken a battalion to stop you." He watched Paulo crossing the glade toward Marna. "However, have you noticed that Marna does resemble a battalion on the march at times?" He turned to Sandor. "What's next for you? Will you go with us to Switzerland?"

Sandor shook his head. "I'll join my men in the hills as quickly as possible. Naldona will be sending emissaries to try to pull the fringe factions loyal to me into his camp, and sending strike forces to the core groups to destroy them before they're aware of the split between us." His expression was grave. "You know that it won't be safe for Marna and her people in the hills. It's not going to be either pleasant or safe for anyone in Tamrovia for a long time."

"War?" Kira asked.

He nodded somberly, making a violent motion with his hand. "I'd almost rather have Stefan back than have Tamrovia go through this hell."

"Where is Stefan? You said he was safe, but you didn't tell me what's happened to him."

"I had an inkling from reports I'd received that Naldona was going to try to make an example of the royal family. Before he reached the palace I took Stefan prisoner myself and had two of my men smuggle him out of Belajo. They should be in Sedikhan by now. I told my men to deliver Stefan to Lance Rubinoff. Hopefully, your brother Lance will be able to convince him not to try to reenter Tamrovia at once." He shrugged. "After a day or so there won't be any question of his coming back. Naldona will have announced the takeover." Sandor's lips tightened. "And I will have launched the first offensive against Naldona's new regime. Stefan will know it will be suicide to come back."

"Poor Stefan," Kira said softly. "I know you said he was a dinosaur and I believe that's true. But the pomp and circumstance of being king is all he's ever known and enjoyed."

"Perhaps he'll be forced to develop into something more now," Zack said quietly. "And if not, deposed kings have a great social cachet in society. There's a certain tragic romanticism about them. He'll probably have just as many sycophants around him as he did in Tamrovia." He turned to Sandor. "I'll fly you to your base now, if you like. You obviously want to join your men immediately."

Sandor nodded. "It's urgent that I do so. It's not very far from here. It shouldn't take you more than an hour to get there and back." He hesitated. "Don't linger here for more than five or six hours at the most. Everyone knows about Kira's association with Marna and her tribe. Naldona will have troops out interrogating and scouring the countryside for the caravans. The Gypsies should break camp and move farther up into the hills, and the two of you should get out of the country before all hell breaks loose."

"Will the tribe be in danger?" Kira asked anxiously.

"Very likely. There will be fighting, and innocent bystanders are never immune in a situation like this." Sandor's lips twisted. "And Naldona's interrogation methods won't be gentle if he decides to question them about your whereabouts."

Kira hurriedly opened the door of the helicopter. "I'll talk to Paulo and Marna and see if we can't get everyone packed up and ready to move out before you get back, Zack." She held out her hand. "Good luck, Sandor. I think you know how grateful I am to you for saving my life. I'm sorry we weren't able to get to know each other before this."

Sandor's strong, warm hand enveloped her own. "So am I." His sudden smile held a hint of amusement. "I'm sure we'll meet again. We think alike. I have an idea we're soul mates, cousin mine."

"Soul mates!" She made a face. "Not you too? My soul certainly appears to be a gregarious rascal."

Sandor frowned in puzzlement. "What?"

"Never mind," Kira said, laughing. "Zack can explain all about soul mates and *mondavas* to you on the way to your base. We've become experts on both lately." She turned to Zack and kissed him with a fierceness that startled him. "You take care of yourself. I want you back here safe and sound in an hour. And no more dodging bullets, do you hear?"

The slightest smile broke the gravity of his face. "Yes, ma'am. I'll try to keep that in mind."

"See that you do." She was blinking furiously as she jumped from the helicopter to the ground. She would not cry. Nothing could happen to Zack now. Surely the worst was over. Yet this self-admonition did very little to loosen the fear that was clawing at her, and she felt tears brimming in her eyes. She didn't want to be parted from him now, dammit. She had been so close to losing him in those woods tonight. All she wanted to do was run off with him somewhere. She wanted to hide and hold him until the realization finally sank in that he was safe and blessedly alive. No, that was a child's reaction and she mustn't give in to it. She must get on with her responsibilities and release Zack to do his.

She forced herself to smile and to lift her hand in a jaunty salute. Then she slammed the door and turned to walk toward Paulo and Marna. She heard the engine start, but didn't turn around to see the helicopter lift off.

Paulo's sympathetic gaze was raking her tense face and glittering eyes. "He's taking Karpathan to his men?"

She nodded silently.

"Nothing will happen to him. Zack is very strong and so is Karpathan." His lips curved in a curious smile. "An interesting man, that Karpathan. I would like to go hunting with him sometime."

She shivered. Karpathan would be the deadliest of hunters and the civil unrest in which he had involved himself would offer ample opportunity to display that lethal talent.

"You think he would have the qualifications you demand in your hunting companions?" Her voice was still a little ragged, despite her attempt at lightness.

Paulo tilted her chin up so that he could look into her eyes. His big calloused hand was as gentle as his gaze. "I just might decide to take you along the next trip, little one. You have learned one of those qualities very well."

"When to let go?" She shook her head. "I haven't learned it very well at all. I want to scream and stamp my feet and howl at the moon."

"But you are not doing any of those things, and you *did* let him go. That is what is important."

"What is important is getting Kira back to camp and getting her something to eat," Marna said crossly. "And you are not to take her hunting, Paulo. You never know when to stop. You would have her starved and exhausted before you brought her home."

"I'm afraid there won't be any hunting for any-one in the near future." Kira was abruptly jarred back to the realities of the situation. "We have to pack up and move the tribe farther into the hills. Sandor said it would be very dangerous for you to stay here. There's going to be a war, Marna."

"So? Will it stop the war if you do without dinner?"

Paulo's deep chuckle boomed out. "Give in, little one, we will go nowhere until she's satisfied."

"But there's no time. How can you be so calm? The war will—"

Marna stopped her with an abrupt gesture of her hand. "There are always wars. Lands are invaded, old governments fall, new governments rise. Everything changes." She tapped her breast with her fist. "Everything but us. We stay the same. That is our strength."

Yes, that was the strength of her people, Kira thought, traditional values which didn't change with each waft of the wind, but stood firm through the centuries. Kira shook her head in resignation. "All right. While I eat, you pack. Is it a deal?"

"Of course." Marna's brows lifted in surprise. "That is very sensible. When have I ever been anything but practical?"

"Never." Kira stood on tiptoe to brush a light kiss on her broad cheek. Magic and strength and love. For Marna, these qualities defined practicality, and who was to say that she wasn't right? She linked her arm through Marna's and urged her gently back toward the encampment. "You're quite right. No one in the world is more pragmatic than you."

Ten

Kira lifted the two-year-old back into his parents' wagon, pressing a kiss on the delicious chubbiness of his cheek as she did so. "Stay there," she warned sternly. It was the third time he had crawled out of the caravan since they had started packing up and breaking camp. Chirak appeared to delight in getting underfoot, and she could tell by the gleam in his bright, dancing eyes that he would probably do it again as soon as her back was turned.

She turned around, her gaze raking the camp. It was almost done. The fire had been extinguished, the horses hitched to the wagons, and each family's belongings carefully packed in its caravan. Even the *saldana* caravan had been pulled over to join the others in the encampment. They were nearly ready for departure and still Zack hadn't come back.

Her worried gaze lifted to the moonlit sky. She had been working feverishly to try to block out the fear, and the moment she stopped, panic began to rise in her again.

"He will return soon. It has not been that long."

Kira turned to where Marna was standing a few feet away. "Three hours. What could he be doing for *three* hours?"

Marna shrugged. "He will tell us when he comes back."

If he comes b— No, she wouldn't think that. Marna was right, he'd be here any minute. "Are you ready to leave? Zack will want to take off again as soon as he arrives."

Marna was silent for a long moment. "I am ready." She paused again. "But I am not going with you."

Kira wasn't even surprised. She knew that somewhere deep inside she had been half-expecting this reaction. "You never did intend to go, did you? From the moment we crossed back from Sedikhan you planned to stay with them."

Marna slowly nodded. "I have a place with them."

"You have a place with me." Kira's eyes were glittering with unshed tears. "I *love* you, dammit."

"But you do not need me. The *mondava* is completed. You are a woman now, in heart as well as in body." Marna gestured, her hand encompassing both the camp and the people bustling cheerfully around them. "*They* need me. The times may not be good again for a long while. We will have to hold fast to each other."

"That's what I want to do to you—hold fast," Kira said huskily.

The tiniest smile tugged at Marna's lips. "But you will not do it. You have learned to let go, remember?"

Kira was silent, fighting tears. "No, I won't do it. Not if that's what you want." She gave up the battle and two tears rolled slowly down her cheeks. "I love you, Marna Debuk."

Marna's big hands cradled Kira's cheeks and she kissed her very gently on the forehead. "And I love you, Kira Rubinoff. You will always be with me."

"I will always be with you," Kira said softly. "As you'll always be with me." She drew a shaky breath. "This is so stupid. We sound like this is forever. I won't accept a lifelong separation. Absolutely not. I'm going to find a way for us to be together, and not only in spirit, dammit."

"We will see," Marna said noncommittally. Her head lifted suddenly, her gaze on the sky. "He is here."

"He is?" Kira's heart gave a leap of relief and joy. She still couldn't hear the familiar whir, but she didn't doubt the statement. "Oh, thank God."

Marna released her and stepped back. "Go to him. I have work to finish."

The helicopter was coming down as she reached the glade, and by the time she had run across it, Zack was opening the door. She leaped into his arms and held on tight. Her face was buried in his chest and her voice was a little muffled. "You're late. Why the devil are you so late? I was so scared, so worried . . ." Her voice trailed off. Oh, dear heaven, how she loved him. He was here. Safe.

"We ran into a little trouble." Zack was smoothing her tangled curls with gentle hands. "Or I would have been back a long time ago."

She lifted her head swiftly. "What trouble?"

"Bullets," he said succinctly. "I had to refuel the helicopter when I reached Sandor's base. Naldona evidently isn't wasting any time. Sandor's base was raided before I could take off again. It was over an hour before Sandor's men managed to fight them off and I was able to get out of there." He smiled. "I'm sorry I wasn't able to obey your orders about staying out of the line of fire. These things just seem to happen in Tamrovia." He kissed her lightly and then stepped back and turned her toward the encampment. "It's time we said our good-byes and got out of here. Are Paulo and his people ready to move up into the hills?"

"Almost." She didn't look at him, but her hand unconsciously sought his. "Marna's going with them."

Zack's fingers threaded through hers in warm, silent support. He didn't speak for a moment. "I was wondering if she would."

"I'll miss her so."

"Yes."

"It's not safe for her, Zack. Sandor said Naldona knew about Marna." She bit her lower lip. "I'm so worried about her. She may not be safe from him even up in the hills."

"Sandor told me he'd have his men try to keep watch over the tribe."

"It sounds like Sandor will have trouble just looking after himself." There was another silence.

"I can't make her choices, can I? She's got the right to do as she thinks best."

"Yes."

Her voice was suddenly violent. "You don't have to agree with me. I don't want to leave her here, dammit. I don't want to be reasonable and mature."

"I know you don't."

"I can see your Indian side is dominating at the moment. You're being very taciturn." She shook her head ruefully. "One of these days I will have evolved to the point where I don't blow apart when something like this happens."

"I hope not." Zack's voice was velvet soft. "Why do you think Marna and I have tried to protect you from the realities all these years? You have a very special gift for caring with every atom of your being. That's a joy for those around you, but it makes you vulnerable. It's also making the pain you're feeling now more intense."

They were entering the encampment and his eyes suddenly narrowed speculatively. "It's true you have no right to interfere, but perhaps—"

Kira's brow knotted in puzzlement. "Perhaps, what?"

He slowly shook his head. "Let me think about it." He released her hand. "There's not much time left. Why don't you spend it with Marna? I'll help Paulo and the men with the last of the heavy loading."

Only Paulo and Marna's wagon remained in the deserted clearing. The rest of the wagons were moving slowly toward the rough dirt road a mile or two from the encampment.

Marna gave Kira a brief, brisk hug. "Everything has been said between us," she said gruffly. "Joy, Kira."

Yes, everything had been said and what was left didn't need words. Kira, too, refused to say good-bye. She kept her voice steady despite its huski-ness. "Joy, Marna."

She watched Marna climb up onto the high seat of the wagon. The tears were brimming as she stepped back beside Zack, who was shaking hands with Paulo.

Paulo turned and smiled down at her. "Don't look so tragic, little Kira. We can't really be parted. Marna has taught you that." He bent and kissed her cheek. "Joy, Kira."

She threw her arms around him and hugged him with all her strength. "Take care, Paulo."

"Always," he said lightly as he climbed onto the wagon seat and picked up the reins. He flicked the reins and the horses began to move forward. They had gone only twenty yards or so when Paulo's head suddenly swiveled and he shouted back at them. "Bighorn sheep? You are sure, Zack?"

Zack grinned. "I'm sure, Paulo."

A wide smile lit Paulo's bearded face and his booming laugh rang out. Then he turned back once again to face the distant road. He slapped the reins and the wagon rolled forward.

"What was that about?" Kira asked.

"I was telling Paulo about some land I've leased from the government in Montana and Idaho." Zack's gaze was on the fast-disappearing wagon.

"A wild country tract about the size of Tamrovia, overflowing with mountains and streams and game. I invited Paulo, Marna, and the tribe to come over for a year or so and see how they like it."

Kira held her breath. "And?"

"He said he'd think about it. Kira, it's only a possibility. There aren't any real certainties in this world, only possibilities. You can't make choices for the people you love, but you can sometimes expand those choices and offer them alternatives."

Kira's face was illuminated with excitement. "They'll come. I know they'll come. Oh, Zack, I was so worried about them."

"There's no guarantee that if they do come, they'll stay. This is their homeland and they may become restless and want to return to it," Zack said. "You have to face facts, Kira."

"But by that time maybe the war will be over and they'll at least be safe." Kira slipped into his arms and burrowed her head in his chest. "But can you get the whole tribe out of Tamrovia?"

"It would take a major airlift. I guess I'd better tell Dubliss to stay put in Switzerland for a while," Zack said, his voice threaded with humor. "I don't think we could get them to leave either their wagons or their horses behind. But the airlift is a definite possibility. I got Paulo to chart their new location on my map, and I told him he could send word through Sandor anytime he felt the need to take a little hunting trip."

"I want to go to Montana as soon as we get back," Kira said eagerly. "I'll take hundreds of pictures of mountains and streams and bighorn sheep and send them to Paulo and Marna." She glanced up, her eyes twinkling. "A letter bombardment seemed to work pretty well for Marna with you. Now we'll just see how she likes it."

Zack nodded. "A masterly plan, love. We'll deluge them with choices and hope they'll make the one that will suit us best."

"Is that an Indian philosophy?" Kira grinned.

"No, the Indian part of me is looking askance at such contrivance." Zack shrugged. "But what can you expect from someone who is neither fish nor fowl?"

She went still. "I know what I expect," she said slowly. "I expect what you always give me: Honesty, strength, intelligence, patience, affection, loyalty . . . Shall I go on?"

He shook his head. "Much as I appreciate the accolades you're heaping on me, I think we'd better dispense with them for the moment. We've been here too long already. We'd better head for the helicopter."

"A few more minutes won't hurt." She leaned back in his arms to look up at him. "I think there are a few things we should get straight. When I first saw you I thought you were the strongest, most confident man I'd ever laid eyes on. I still think that, but I believe you have one major hang-up, Zack."

His eyes studied her face. "And what is that?"

"The same one that's been the bane of my existence all these years. My damn title." She lifted her hand to stop him as he began to speak. "No, I know you don't have any desire to gain status through it, but it's a bugaboo just the same. I think my title intimidates you."

"Intimidates?"

"Remember when you told me about discounting the possibility that a princess and a half-breed could ever really get together, when Marna first told you about the *mondava*? You didn't even question that reaction. And why didn't you go after me when you decided you wanted me, instead of waiting for Marna to serve me up to you on a silver platter?" She drew a deep breath. "And why haven't you asked me to marry you? I know you love me. You were angry when you thought I wasn't going through with the *mondava*, but you never even suggested that we be linked together in a ceremony joining us in the eyes of the world. In some ways, I think you never recovered from those experiences that scarred you as a child." She paused deliberately. "You're a half-breed, and a bastard, and heaven only knows who some of your antecedents were, Zack Damon. You're also the finest, most wonderful man I've ever met. So who the hell *cares*?"

"There's a possibility you may be right about my hang-up. I guess I never thought about it. I just reacted." Zack was looking at her with eyes glowing with intensity. "Who the hell cares?" he echoed thickly. "Will you marry me, Kira?"

"You bet I will." She threw her arms around his neck and hugged him ecstatically. "Oh, Zack, I do love you so much. I was afraid you might be going to turn noble on me and want to leave me free or something. There's been so much talk of that lately." She kissed him. "Now listen carefully. I do *not* want to be free. I want to belong to you and to have you belong to me. I know that you would never try to stifle me, just as I would never try to stifle you." Her gaze was fixed earnestly on his face. "But I want the marriage tie between us. I believe in it. Call it the *mondava* or just plain love. It exists, Zack, and it will exist for the rest of our lives."

"I know." He leaned forward to kiss her gently. "And even longer than the rest of our lives. The everlasting bonding. We're very lucky to have found it, and we'd be damned fools to risk losing it." He kissed her again with a power and passion that was a shining promise. Then he lifted his head and his voice was a little unsteady. "I love you, Kira. I'll love you forever."

The moment was so fraught with beauty and meaning that she couldn't speak.

At last he released her. "More later," he said with a low, husky laugh. He took her elbow. "Now, let's get out of here before Naldona's soldiers come breathing down our necks."

He didn't speak again until they had lifted off and were flying north over the dark forests and moonlit ribboned streams. He glanced at her searchingly. "You're very quiet. Are you very unhappy about leaving your home?"

Kira lifted her eyes from the rolling panorama below. Yes, it was sad to be leaving, particularly when she wanted so desperately to help Tamrovia. Yet Zack had said there would be ways for them to help in the struggle, and she knew together they would find those ways. In the final analysis, from now on wherever Zack was, her home would be, just as she would be the lodestone of his existence.

She held out her left hand and he took it and clasped it with warm, comforting strength.

"I'm not leaving home." She smiled at him lovingly. "I'm going home, Zack. I'm *going* home."

THE EDITOR'S CORNER

Do you grumble as much as I do about there being too few hours in the day? Time. There just never seems to be enough of it! That seemed especially to be the case a few weeks ago when we were sitting here facing a scheduling board with every slot filled for months and months . . . and an embarrassment of goodies (finished LOVESWEPT manuscripts, of course). But, then, suddenly, it occurred to us that the real world limitations of days and months didn't necessarily apply to a publishing schedule. Voilà! 1986 got rearranged a bit as we created a thirteenth month in the year for a unique LOVESWEPT publishing event. Our thirteenth month features three special romances going on sale October 15, 1986.

What's so remarkable that it warrants the creation of a month? Another "first" in series romance from LOVESWEPT: A trio of love stories by three of your favorite LOVESWEPT authors—Fayrene Preston, Kay Hooper, and Iris Johansen. **THE SHAMROCK TRINITY!** Fayrene, Kay, and Iris together "founded" the Delaney dynasty—its historical roots, principal members, settings, and present day heirs. (Those heirs are three of the most exciting men you'd ever want to meet in the pages of romances—Burke, York, and Rafe.) Armed with genealogies, sketches of settings, research notes they'd made on a joint trip to Arizona in which the books were to be set, each author then went off alone to create her own book in her own special style. There are common secondary characters, running gags through the three books. They can be read in any order, stand alone if the other two books are not read. Each book features appearances by the heroes of the other two books, each is set during the same span of time—and yet, no one gives away the end of the other books. This is a fascinating trinity of stories, indeed, very clever and well-crafted, and packing all the wallop you expect in a love story by Fayrene or Kay or Iris.

Don't miss these extraordinary love stories. Ask your bookseller to be sure to save the three books of **THE SHAMROCK TRINITY** for you. They are:

RAFE, THE MAVERICK
LOVESWEPT #167
By Kay Hooper

(continued)

YORK, THE RENEGADE
LOVESWEPT #168
By Iris Johansen

BURKE, THE KINGPIN
LOVESWEPT #169
By Fayrene Preston

Now, as I said above, there is an embarrassment of goodies around here. And four excellent examples are your LOVESWEPT romances for next month.

Leading off is witty Billie Green with **GLORY BOUND,** LOVESWEPT #155. Gloria Wainwright had a secret . . . and Alan Spencer, a blind date arranged by her matchmaking father, was a certain threat to keeping that secret. He was just too darned attractive, too irresistible, and the only way to maintain her "other life" was for Glory to avoid him—in fact, to disappear from Alan's world. But he tracked down the elusive lady whose various disguises hadn't repelled him as Glory intended, but only further intrigued him. When Alan and Glory come face to face in her bedroom—under the wildest circumstances imaginable—firecrackers truly do go off between these two. This romance is another sheer delight from Billie Green.

After a long absence from our list, the versatile Marie Michael is back with **NO WAY TO TREAT A LOVER,** LOVESWEPT #156. This is the fastpaced, exciting—often poignant—love story of beautiful Charley (short for Charlotte) Tremayne and the deliciously compelling Reese McDaniel. After a madly passionate affair, Charley had disappeared to follow a dangerous life of intrigue. Now, she and Reese are thrown together again on the stage of a musical bound for Broadway. Charley tries to stay away from Reese—for his safety!—but cannot resist him! You'll want to give both of these endearing people a standing ovation as they overcome Charley's fears . . . and a few other stumbling blocks fate throws in their way.

Peggy Webb's **DUPLICITY,** LOVESWEPT #157, is a delightfully humorous book that also will tug at your heartstrings. Dr. Ellen Stanford knows it is reckless to bring a perfect stranger home to pose as her fiance, but she just can't face another family reunion alone. Besides, the myste-

(continued)

rious Dirk is about as perfect as a man can get—as good looking as Tom Selleck, masterful yet tender, and one fabulous kisser! But Ellen is dedicated to her work, teaching sign language to a gorilla named Gigi, and Dirk is pledged to a way of life filled with dangerous secrets. How Dirk and Ellen work through their various deceptions will delight you and no doubt make you laugh out loud—especially when Gigi gets in the act as matchmaker!

Rounding out the month is another fabulous romance from Barbara Boswell! **ALWAYS AMBER,** LOVESWEPT #158, is a sequel to **SENSUOUS PERCEPTION,** LOVE-SWEPT #78. Remember Ashlee and Amber? They were the twins who were adopted in infancy by different families. In **SENSUOUS PERCEPTION,** Ashlee located her sister—and fell in love with Amber's brother. Now it's Amber's turn for romance. She has finally broken out of her shell and left the family banking business. The last person she expects to meet, much less be wildly attracted to, is Jared Stone, president of a bank that is her family's biggest rival. Amber doesn't quite trust Jared's intentions toward her, but can't deny her overwhelming need for him. You'll cheer Jared on as he passionately, relentlessly pursues Amber, until he finally breaks through her last inhibitions. . . . A breathless, delicious love story!

At long—wonderful—last the much awaited **SUNSHINE AND SHADOW** by Sharon and Tom Curtis will be published. This fabulous novel will be on sale during the first week of September. Be sure to look for it.

Have a glorious month of reading pleasure!

Warm regards,

Sincerely,

Carolyn Nichols

Carolyn Nichols
   Editor
LOVESWEPT
Bantam Books, Inc.
666 Fifth Avenue
New York, NY 10103

LOVESWEPT

Love Stories you'll never forget by authors you'll always remember

LOVESWEPT

Love Stories you'll never forget by authors you'll always remember

☐	21760	**Donovan's Angel #143** Peggy Webb	$2.50
☐	21761	**Wild Blue Yonder #144** Millie Grey	$2.50
☐	21762	**All Is Fair . . . #145** Linda Cajio	$2.50
☐	21763	**Journey's End #146** Joan Elliott Pickart	$2.50
☐	21751	**Once In Love With Amy #147** Nancy Holder	$2.50
☐	21749	**Always #148** Iris Johansen	$2.50
☐	21765	**Time After Time #149** Kay Hooper	$2.50
☐	21767	**Hot Tamales #150** Sara Orwig	$2.50

Prices and availability subject to change without notice.

Buy them at your local bookstore or use this handy coupon for ordering:

BANTAM
SHOP-AT-HOME
C·A·T·A·L·O·G

Special Offer
Buy a Bantam Book
for only 50¢.

Now you can have an up-to-date listing of Bantam's hundreds of titles plus take advantage of our unique and exciting bonus book offer. A special offer which gives you the opportunity to purchase a Bantam book for only 50¢. Here's how!

By ordering any five books at the regular price per order, you can also choose any other single book listed (up to a $4.95 value) for just 50¢. Some restrictions do apply, but for further details why not send for Bantam's listing of titles today!

Just send us your name and address and we will send you a catalog!
